SARAH KILLIAN

THE MULLETS OF MADNESS

A Novel By

MARK SHELDON

Let the world know:
#IGotMyCLPBook!

Crystal Lake Publishing
www.CrystalLakePub.com

Be sure to sign up for our newsletter and receive
a free eBook: http://eepurl.com/xfuKP

ISBN: 978-1-64633-858-0

Cover Art:
Ben Baldwin—www.benbaldwin.co.uk

Layout:
Lori Michelle—www.theauthorsalley.com

Edited by:
Monique Snyman

Proofread by:
Kat Nava

SET YOUR
IMAGINATION
FREE!

Welcome to another Crystal Lake Publishing creation.

Thank you for supporting independent publishing and small presses. You rock, and hopefully you'll quickly realize why we've become one of the world's leading publishers of Dark and Speculative Fiction. We have some of the world's best fans for a reason, and hopefully we'll be able to add you to that list really soon. Be sure to sign up for our newsletter to receive some free eBooks, as well as info on new releases, special offers, and so much more.

We'd like to specifically thank Stephen C. Ormsby, John J. Questore, Faith Dincolo, Brandy Yassa, Carrie Clevenger, Darryl Foster, Steve Pattee, Sarah Read, Nick Zinn, Amy Drees, Matt Neil Hill, Elke Flehmig, Dan Howarth, Terry M Weyna, Andrea Rawson, Christa Miller, Geoffrey Young Haney, Jeffrey Dick, Kenneth Skaldebø, and James K Chambliss.

**Welcome to Crystal Lake Publishing—
Tales from the Darkest Depths.**

OTHER NOVELS BY CRYSTAL LAKE PUBLISHING

Or check out other Crystal Lake Publishing books for more Tales from the Darkest Depths.

"I like killing people because it is so much fun. It is more fun than killing wild game in the forest because man is the most dangerous animal of them all."

—The Zodiac Killer

1

DO WE REALLY have to go through this whole 'introduce ourselves' thing again? The only thing I hate more than introductions is repeating myself.

Okay, okay. Fine. I'll do this, though I have to say it would be easier for all of us if you just read my first book.

So, my name is Sarah Killian and I am a Professional Serial Killer. DO NOT confuse me with an *ass*assin. I hate those guys. Every. Last. One.

Well, except for Mary Sue. She's an exception. She's an exception to a lot of things. I'll get to *her* in a bit.

In a tortoise shell, I work for a secret organization known as T.H.E.M.—the Trusted Hierarchy of Everyday Murderers. T.H.E.M. is clandestinely contracted by private individuals, corporations, or sometimes even the government to complete the dirty work of furtively killing off individuals or groups of people.

I won't bother covering the *ass*assin side of things, because that's pretty much just the boring, run-of-the-mill shit you've seen in every Hollywood movie.

SNORE. No, the interesting side of T.H.E.M. operations is my side—the Professional Serial Killers, or P.S.K.'s.

Basically, when a client of T.H.E.M. wants to wipe out a large group of people discreetly, a P.S.K. gets sent in, under cover, to make it look like it was the work of a serial killer. The P.S.K. positions themselves in the community for several months, sometimes even years, and creates a profile of the killer they will be portraying—the 'Herring.' Sometimes the Herring is one of the marks that will be killed, and at the end of the mission the P.S.K. will make it look as if the Herring killed themselves. Other times, the Herring is a completely fictitious persona invented by the P.S.K. who, at the end of the killing spree, will disappear into the void from whence they came –a la Jack the Ripper or the Zodiac Killer.

But that's not all, not only does the P.S.K. have to stage the persona of the Herring, but they also have the 'Dupe'—the 'everyday' person they are pretending to be while on assignment. If the Herring is not one of the Marks, the Dupe and the Herring could be one and the same—however that's generally avoided as you don't want to draw too much attention to your Dupe character. The Dupe ideally is someone who just blends into the background of the killing spree and does not attract any extra scrutiny from the authorities or public eye.

But it's even more complicated than *that*. Not only on each mission does the P.S.K. have to maintain at least two separate personae, but they also have to be able to make each and every case they take *completely* different, to prevent the Feds (or amateur investigators) from being able to connect the dots and realize multiple cases are the work of one person.

As you can imagine, this line of work is ideal for people with multiple personalities.

As for getting recruited into T.H.E.M., obviously it's not the kind of thing where you can go to a job fair and fill out an application. That would be silly.

In order to get hired by T.H.E.M., you first have to get on their radar. Kill five people without being identified or caught, and you've got T.H.E.M.'s attention, even if they don't know exactly who you are yet. This earns you the label of a Recognized but Unidentified Serial Killer (R.U.S.K.), meaning T.H.E.M. has identified your killings are the work of one person, they just don't know who you are. Kill ten people without getting *caught*, and T.H.E.M. will try to recruit you—obviously they'll have to have identified you before they can recruit you, but T.H.E.M. is *very* good at identifying serial killers, so if you kill more than ten people without getting identified by T.H.E.M., you are something special. I used to think I was pretty special, because I had killed thirteen people before T.H.E.M. caught up with me.

Then I met Mary Sue. She killed twenty (or twenty-one—she's a bit hazy on that matter) people before T.H.E.M. approached her. Fucking Mary Sue.

Sorry, did I mention I have Tourette's? No? Well, I have fucking Tourette's, so you might as well get fucking used to me fucking swearing, fucking got it?

Sorry. Like I said, Tourette's.

Anyway, kill more than ten people without being caught by the Feds, and once T.H.E.M. has successfully identified you they will come to you with an offer: work for T.H.E.M. as a P.S.K., and they will have your official record expunged and you will be immune from prosecution for the rest of your life. Reject their offer, and they immediately hand you over to the Feds.

'How can they make such a promise?' you might ask. Remember how I mentioned earlier the Government is one of our biggest clients? Yeah, that's how.

Obviously, if you've murdered more than ten people, and get offered a deal like that, most people will take the deal. There is, however, a catch. You have to stop killing for pleasure. Cold turkey. One single murder outside of a T.H.E.M. assignment, and your ass is grass, baby. Your contract with T.H.E.M. will be nullified and you get to spend your last remaining days in a padded room waiting to find out if you get put down by lethal injection.

But really, that one caveat is not too much to ask, especially since if I ever get a sudden urge to kill, I can just contact my boss—Zeke—and he's good at finding quick work to satisfy my craving for blood.

I was twenty-two when Zeke approached me, and like I said I had killed thirteen people at that point, so his offer was a no-brainer. Zeke is, as a matter-of-fact, the original founder of T.H.E.M. and something of a mystery. A disgusting slob of a mystery, but a mystery nonetheless. All I *really* know about him is that he used to be a serial killer, but then he 'retired' and founded T.H.E.M..

To get a picture of Zeke physically, imagine the progeny of the union of Ron Jeremy, Barry Williams, and a seriously obese walrus. In short, just about the only thing going for him physically is his black curly hair—curly hair is a weakness of mine, and it's the only thing that keeps me from wanting to vomit whenever I see him. I still won't touch the man with a thirty-foot pole if I can help it, but at least I don't want to kill him, which would definitely void my contract.

Maybe I'm just a disturbed sociopath, but this was actually the perfect job for me. Well, until four months, ago that is.

I got called onto a job in Duluth, Minnesota. It was just going to be a standard Zoo Project (i.e.: go to a high school, kill a bunch of dumb-fuck teenagers, etc.), but at the last minute Zeke slapped me with a trainee— Mary Sue, or Bethany as I knew her at the time. At first, this was not the most welcome of news I could have received. I do *not* play well with others— especially when those 'others' are obnoxious, bubbly, annoying, blonde bimbos like Mary Sue.

However—although I hate to admit it—I probably would not be alive to tell you this had she not been with me on that assignment.

As it transpired, 'Bethany' was an *ass*assin, who Zeke had assigned to me because a former employee of T.H.E.M., Nick Jin, had broken out of prison and gone rogue. Zeke, in his infinite paranoia, was worried that Nick—who was something of a disgruntled former employee—would attempt to interfere with T.H.E.M. operatives in the field.

As it turned out, Zeke was right on the money, because barely even a month into my assignment in Duluth, Nick showed up and started killing people in a convoluted scheme worthy of M. Night Shyamalamadingdong order to draw my attention so he could try and recruit me into his crusade to bring down T.H.E.M.. Did I mention that Nick is a raving lunatic? No? Well, he is. Several years ago, the guy went over the deeper end and had a complete and very public psychotic break, almost exposing T.H.E.M. in the process. Fortunately, the rest of the world dismissed his babbling as the ravings of a paranoid lunatic and no one took him seriously.

In any event, Nick cornered me and asked me to join him and his mystery accomplice, I declined the offer and threw Nick out of the window of a tower (Ok, ok. Yes . . . he also gave me a pretty significant ass-kicking before I threw him out of the aforementioned window. Sheesh, why don't ya just focus on the insignificant details, already . . .) Unfortunately, the bastard survived and disappeared into the void from whence he came.

Oh yeah, the fuck-tard also tricked me into sleeping with him by disguising himself as a T.H.E.M. I.T. operative who bore a striking resemblance to David Brennan, a celebrity crush of mine and former star of the Sci-fi TV series *Mr. What*. I'd rather not admit that tiny detail, but if I didn't tell you about it, Mary Sue probably would and she'd undoubtedly embellish it to the utmost point of embarrassment, so there you have it.

If all of the other bullshit Nick Jin put me through didn't make me want to plunge a sharp, cold knife into his soft, moist gut, *that* tactic certainly put the jackass on my top list of people to kill. Who else is on the list? Well, aside from pretty much *all of humanity*, Michael Bay for crimes against '80's and '90's pop culture, and Winona Ryder for being a brat.

Ever since that run-in with Nick, I have been taking informal daily martial arts lessons from Mary Sue. One major difference between *ass*assins and P.S.K.'s is *ass*assins are fully trained in martial arts. I'd never really had an interest in martial arts before, but after getting my ass handed to me by Nick in Duluth, I reluctantly admitted it might be a worthwhile skill to take up, because even before he joined T.H.E.M. as an *ass*assin he was already a deadly martial arts expert. I didn't *want* to have to see Mary Sue anymore than absolutely necessary, but there's really only one other *ass*assin whose identity I know, and let's just say that *he* is not an option. And yes, *that* is all I am going to say on that matter.

So, I think that should more or less bring you up to speed. I kill people for a living, and like it. Zeke is my disgusting boss. Mary Sue is an obnoxious burden to whom I owe my very life. And Nick Jin is conspiring to bring T.H.E.M. down and anyone who stands in his way—namely me.

I still say it would've been easier if you'd just read the first book.

2

HAVE YOU EVER woken up some morning with a burning, insatiable desire to go out and kill someone? No? Huh. Guess I'm weird, then.

Anyway, this morning I wake up with such a craving. As usual, the craving has been preceded by a dream—well, a flashback to be exact. It's always the same memory, and if you think I'm going to tell you anymore than that, you really *do* need to go back and read the first book, because you clearly have not yet learned I am the kind of person who will break the fourth wall a couple times every other page, but you will have to torture me (and not the fun kind of torture) before I talk about personal, psycho, feelings shit.

Thanks to my contract with T.H.E.M., I can't exactly just go out and find myself an unsuspecting tourist on Hollywood Blvd. to lure back to a hotel room where I can de-spleen the poor bastard. However, Zeke is generally pretty flexible about finding us short projects whenever we need a quickie.

Technically, one-off jobs (where we only kill one person) are reserved for *ass*assins, since P.S.K.'s focus more on multiple killings and *ass*assins are better suited for 'quick and easy' projects. However from time-to-time Zeke will let the P.S.K.'s take on an easy one-off he doesn't have an *ass*assin immediately available for.

"We all go a little mad sometimes, Marion," Zeke says in an annoying Anthony Perkins impersonation when he answers my phone call. Have I mentioned Zeke likes to creep people out by impersonating famous movie serial killers? Have I mentioned I hate my boss, sometimes? I mean, sure everyone says at some point or another they hate their boss, but when I say it I actually mean I would love nothing more than to take a knife and plunge it deep into his substantial gut. The only things keeping me from acting on it are that I don't want to break my contract with T.H.E.M. and the thought of having to dig through all that blubber in order to actually get at any vital organs is repulsive even to me.

Anyway, I bite back the bile building in the back of my throat and respond, "Good morning, Zeke. I'm in serious need of a quickie."

"Sarah, I'm flattered, but you know I don't consort with my agents," Zeke's slippery voice slithers over the phone line. I can feel my nether region shriveling up and sealing itself shut forever in sheer disgust at the thought of Zeke's insinuation.

"You know what I mean, you fuck-monkey," I snap. For all my complaints about Zeke, I at least have to give him credit for not minding back-talk. I am well aware most bosses would not put up with their employees directly calling them a fuck-monkey.

Zeke lets out an exaggerated sigh, then continues, "Fine, fine. Let me see . . . "

He spends a few seconds pretending to look through his planner, but I know for a fact he has every client and prospective job memorized in that seriously disturbed brain of his. Zeke really is nothing if not an over-dramatic showman. He probably would've gone into Hollywood had he not decided killing people was more fun.

"Let's see, let's see, oh here we go!" The act is enough to make me want to scream, but I bite my tongue, because I really want to kill someone today and I don't want to give Zeke a reason to deny my request. "I've got a senator—Senator Gene Keeley. He has a political rival who wants him offed in a thoroughly humiliating way. Those are your favorites, aren't they?"

I hate to admit to Zeke being right about anything, but yes; taking a skeeze ball politician and publicly revealing him to be the dirt bag he really is, and getting to kill him in the process, definitely falls into the category of my favorite pastimes.

"Gimme the stats," I respond, refusing to give him the satisfaction of confirming he was right.

"Senator Keeley is home from D.C. for the week—arrived this morning. He'll be at City Hall for meetings for most of the day, and if he continues his usual routine—just about the only thing a politician can be counted on—he will be calling his regular . . . *ahem* . . . 'agency' for some off-the-books entertainment before going home to his wife. If you want the job, I will arrange to have his smart phone hacked and that call will be routed to us."

Before you even get it in your head, let me clear this up: no, I will *not* be sleeping with the skuzbasket. I will only be *posing* as an escort to get the bastard alone so I can slice and dice. To be fair, there's nothing in my contract that says I can't sleep with him before doing the deed—all T.H.E.M. cares about is the mark gets killed. What we do with him beforehand is just 'playing with the food,' so to speak. But especially for these jobs where a politician is the mark, I'd prefer not risk contracting every STD known to man, thank you very much.

"I'll take it," I say, probably a tad too-eagerly, but I really need to kill someone—especially a man –before I go over the deeper end.

"Fine. Get here to HQ as soon as possible so the Makeover Specialists can give you a basic treatment. Oh, and Sarah . . . "

"Yes . . . ?" the tone of his voice makes it abundantly clear I am not going to like what's coming next . . .

"You'll be taking Misk with you."

Fuck. Misk, by the way, is Mary Sue's T.H.E.M. code name.

"*Seriously,* Easy?" I snap ('Easy' is my nickname for Zeke, it's about the only thing I can do that irritates him as much as he irritates me). "This is a stupid one-off job, I don't need a baby sitter."

"You know the rules, Sarah," Zeke admonishes. "Ever since your incident last fall, no one—especially you—goes on assignment alone."

I say this several times a day, but if I ever run into Nick Jin again, I am going to murder him. Nice and slow. Preferably with a wiffle bat so it will take extra long to get the job done.

"If you'd prefer someone else," Zeke slithers, "I could always have Ja—"

"Fine," I grumble into the phone cutting him off abruptly. I'd prefer to spend one stupid quickie project working with Mary Sue than even have to hear Jason's name again. Jason is my ex—an *ass*assin who I dated until he cheated on me. Bastard.

"Good girl. Just tell Keeley you're training a newb, so he gets two for the price of one. One last thing, Sarah. Remember that a girl's best friend is her mother."

And the line goes dead. Porcupines, I *hate* that man. Paraphrasing a quote from one of the best horror films of all time to remind me about my mother—*that* is a shot way below the belt.

Fuck, I guess this means I need to tell you about my mother now. For the love of Captain Hammer's nipples, I really hate Zeke sometimes.

Alright. Long story short, when I was sixteen my mother killed my deadbeat father for beating the two of us up on a regular basis. Instead of getting a Mother of the Year Medal, she got thrown in jail and I became a child of the state. To this day, she resides in Los Angeles County Prison, and she does not—nor will she ever—know I work as a serial killer for hire. As far as she knows, I work as an office assistant for a high-profile law firm that has offices across the country and frequently sends me out-of-state to other branches for special cases.

Zeke knows all of this and uses it as leverage against me—if I ever step out of line on an assignment, he just reminds me that he will tell my mother what I do, and the thought of her broken heart is enough to force me to stay in line.

Zeke's prodding elicits the usual rage-induced

response in me: I calmly go to my second walk-in closet, which is stocked floor-to-ceiling with cute, fluffy, stuffed animals, and pick out a particularly fluffy bunny with annoyingly big blue eyes that would put Frank Sinatra to shame. I calmly return to my bedroom and tape a picture of Zeke onto the face of the unsuspecting thumper. I calmly lift up a corner of my mattress and take out my favorite knife—the same knife I made my first kill with all those years ago. Finally abandoning all pretense of calmness, I unleash my rage on the cutesy cottontail.

Fluff and fabric swirl around me in a hurricane of flurry, but in my mind's eye it is not stuffing and fake fur, but blood and guts that pollute my surroundings.

Also, even though it is Zeke's face taped to the coney, it is not his face I see. As always, it is another, and as always my rage is only left half-quenched by the time I am spent.

3

NORMALLY BEFORE I go on an assignment, I would pay my mother a visit. It's really just about the only time I visit her, which is one of the many reasons I deserve the award for Worst Daughter of All Time (though not the main reason, by a long shot). However, since this isn't exactly going to be a long-term assignment, I decide to put-off the visit and go straight to T.H.E.M. headquarters.

The headquarters are located in Chatsworth at the far-west-end of the San Fernando Valley, in a building the general public assumes to be a porn distribution warehouse. It takes me longer than it might to get to Chatsworth, due to the fact I have to avoid freeways thanks to my 'condition.' See, I have a somewhat rare illness—so rare none of the doctors I've seen about it have ever heard or seen anything like it before. In a nutshell, I'm allergic to radar. *Technically* speaking, it's not really an allergy—just a hypersensitivity. See, radar has this annoying tendency to send me into a mini-seizure.

I'm really not supposed to drive at all—I'm restricted from having a license and everything—but have you ever tried to get anywhere using the Los

Angeles public transportation system? No thank you. As you probably have guessed by now, I kinda like my independence anyway. Besides, as far as my list of sins goes, driving without a license is pretty close to the bottom of the pile.

Anyway, I drive my fire-red Porsche through the somewhat less radar-enforced surface streets across the valley to the headquarters warehouse. I enter the building using my employee I.D. badge, thoroughly ignoring the security guard on duty who undoubtedly thinks I'm there to film some new inventory. On the surface level, the interior of the building looks exactly like a porn distribution warehouse. Rows and rows upon shelves stocked with DVD inventory. I promise you, though, it is not what it seems.

I make my way to the back of the warehouse, to the last shelf of 'inventory.' I scan the rows of DVD cases looking for the current 'code title'—*Alexandra Cameltoe*. I'll be honest, porn doesn't usually 'do it' for me. *Texas Chainsaw Massacre* (the original, not the Michael Douchebay farce remake), sure—but some stupid bimbo college student willing to do *anything* to get a passing grade, or an even dumber but well-hung pizza delivery guy with a 'special delivery? Sorry but that shit doesn't do anything to twix my nethers. That said, I *have* watched *Alexandra Cameltoe*—not for erotic pleasure, but just simply because of the fact that it would literally be impossible *not* to watch a rap opera porn parody about the 'Pounding Sisters.' I mean, the tag line of the movie is 'There's a million guys she hasn't done, but just you wait' and it features such hit songs as *Right Hand Job, The Puss Was Wide Enough, Blow Us All Today, His Story Has His Balls On You,* and—

my personal favorite—*Who Cums, Who Tries, Who Fills Your Glory Hole*. How could I turn that down and still live with myself? Answer: I couldn't.

Anyway, I find the DVD about halfway down the middle shelf, pull it out, setting off the trigger mechanism which causes the shelf to slide aside, revealing a hidden staircase leading down to the basement—the heart of T.H.E.M.'s headquarters.

While the above warehouse is dark, dusty, and cluttered, the underbelly of T.H.E.M.'s operations is almost blindingly white and pristinely clean. Seriously, I'm pretty sure if someone carrying the Ebola virus were to even put one toe in one of T.H.E.M.'s subterranean halls, the virus would scamper out of that person's body and flee for its life, leaving a virus shaped hole in the victim's abdomen in its wake, *a la* Wile E. Coyote.

As I walk through the secret halls, I occasionally pass other T.H.E.M. workers. I don't know them, and they don't know me. Some of them may be P.S.K.'s like me, others may be *ass*assins, and some just paper-pushers who may not even know what T.H.E.M. *really* does. There's really no distinguishing identifier that separates the uniforms of the departments—aside from the people in the white coats. I don't really know what they do, to be honest, but I don't think it makes me a genius to assume that they're some sort of R&D scientists, or something like that.

Anyway, I make my way back to the domain of the F.U.C.K.'s (Fabricating Ugly Cock-Kissers). That's actually not their official title, it's just what I personally call them. I honestly don't even remember what they're actually called anymore . . .

The F.U.C.K.'s are T.H.E.M.'s disguise specialists. What they do is some sort of cross-hybrid of plastic surgery and prosthetic make-up. Don't ask me to explain how it works exactly—I ain't a scientist. If you wanted a science book, you should've picked up something by Neil DeGrasse Tyson. All I know about whatever it is the F.U.C.K.'s do is that it as painful as fuck (hence my nickname for them).

Basically, you go in yourself, and you come out looking like someone completely different. It's a procedure that is not as permanent as actual plastic surgery, but lasts longer than prosthetic make-up and doesn't have to be changed and replaced every day.

For a full-on long-term project, the procedure usually takes around six hours—six hours of the F.U.C.K.'s poking and prodding every inch of your body. Sticking needles where you should never have needles stuck. Stretching you. Twisting you. The F.U.C.K.'s are sadistic bastards, the lot.

They can change your hair pigmentation (with a longer-lasting effect than just your standard over-the-counter hair dye formula), the color of your skin, even the color of your eyes, believe it or not (the injection for that one by far is the worst). Hell, they can even change your gender if you sign on for that (one word: *ew)*. Not full-on gender replacement, mind you, but a good enough passing job so as long as you don't wear spandex or engage in coital relations with anyone while on assignment, no one would suspect a thing. I have no intention of *ever* volunteering for *that* procedure.

I'm pretty sure the F.U.C.K.'s do not fall into the category of people who know what T.H.E.M. is really about—they probably think they work for some secret government espionage agency. Dumb F.U.C.K.'s.

Luckily for me, this time the procedure won't take too long since I'm just going in for a quickie assignment. They don't need to do a full-on make-over—just change enough of my features so that anyone who sees me with my mark or at the location of his death won't be able to identify the real me in a line-up. Incidentally—I actually have been in some line-ups for murders I committed for T.H.E.M. (it's actually kinda common for P.S.K.'s and *ass*assins to volunteer for line-ups just for the sake of having a laugh at the system), and not once have I ever been picked out. I guess I have to give the F.U.C.K.'s credit for *that*, at least.

The quick version only takes an hour and a half, but it still hurts like fuck. My one saving grace is this time there is a woman on my make-over team, so she actually keeps the guys in line and stops them from overdoing it as far as breast augmentation and hip reduction goes. Thank porcupines for small favors.

Her redemption, however, is short lived when, at the end of the session, she says, "Let's give her brown eyes, this time."

Bitch.

After they're done sticking needles in my eyeballs, they put me in an oversized blue t-shirt, take a photograph for the documents forgery department, and then they let me go. Normally at this point I would have an hour-long hot tub soak to look forward to (technically, it has something to do with the process and making sure the modifications settle in properly, but I prefer to overlook that technicality and just focus on the relaxing benefits). Sadly, that will not be necessary today, since I went through the easy-bake option.

As I step out of my F.U.C.K. exam room wearing nothing but a plain white bathrobe (my personal clothes and belongings will be returned to me after my assignment has been completed), a very well-endowed Asian woman steps out of the room next to mine. She takes one look at me, smirks, and says, "I see you were lucky enough to get Jessica on your team, this time, Sick."

If it weren't for that annoying voice (and her use of my codename, 'Sick'—I can count the number of T.H.E.M. operatives who know even just my codename on one hand), I wouldn't even suspect it was Mary Sue—that's how good the F.U.C.K.'s are. There aren't many people who can take a bubbly Barbie-doll Valley girl and turn her into a convincing Asian woman (well-endowed, or otherwise).

"Jessica? I never bother to learn any of their names," I reply. I'm not exactly the type to get chummy with my co-workers. Mary Sue is the one and only exception, and that's only barely since I can only somewhat tolerate even her.

Mary Sue rolls her eyes and sneers, "Why am I not surprised?" She then adapts the worst, most offensive Asian accent I have ever heard, and says, "Werr, gillfliend, you leady to kirr some holny poritician?"

4

AST STOP BEFORE heading out to meet our mark is the wardrobe department. If this were a long-term assignment, the wardrobe workers would have already set aside a full set of clothing, fake I.D.'s, etc. Since this is just a one-off job, however, the wardrobe assistant just leads us to a room with racks and racks of clothes, along the lines of a *Ross Dress for Less* store, and leaves us to our own devices.

While many non-Vegas escort ladies often try to 'stay under the radar' when arriving at a John's location and not be too obvious about their profession, Mary Sue and I have a different priority for our job. We *want* anyone who sees us to assume we are sex workers, and often the best way to put an idea into someone's head is to give them exactly what they expect.

To that end, I pick out the tightest, skimpiest skirt I can find on the rack, and Mary Sue chooses something I suppose is technically a dress, but is more like just a large belt. We each select a pair of stilettos that would make Jack the Giant Killer start chopping down beanstalks if he saw us wearing them.

Our wardrobe selected, we return to the wardrobe counter and sign off for the items we are checking out.

The clerk also hands us two fake I.D.'s—featuring the pictures taken by the F.U.C.K.'s—and two purses containing various tawdry items, some petty cash, and a knife each. My new name is Jessa Monroe, and Mary Sue's is Ming Lee. If those don't both sound like stripper names, then I don't know what does—but as with the wardrobe, it's best to give people exactly what they expect if you want them to assume something.

In the dressing room, I take a look at my 'temporary' self for the first time. I don't care how many times I go through this, I will *never* get used to looking into a mirror and seeing a complete stranger looking back me. My green eyes have been turned brown, my dark brown hair is now platinum blonde, and my skin tone is significantly paler than normal. My cheeks have a bit more lingering baby fat than I'm used to seeing, and although my boobs are slightly larger than normal, I whisper a silent thank you to 'Jessica' for saving me from the enhancement Mary Sue received. Even *I* wouldn't be able to pick myself out of a line-up.

On our way out, we stop at a board that has several pegs with car keys and labels. I select a set labeled 'red '97 convertible' (I like red . . . so kill me . . .), and we proceed back upstairs into the porn warehouse. I can literally feel the eyes of the security guard following us out the door as we step out back into the sunlight.

We cross the parking lot to where the 'company' cars are located and find our temporary red convertible. Mary Sue grabs the keys out of my hand and says, "I'm drivin', sweetie. Last thing we need is to have to take you to the hospital before we've even gotten to the mark."

I roll my eyes in irritation, but don't argue, because even I have to admit she is right. I really don't like admitting that, though.

Almost as soon as we have pulled out of the T.H.E.M. parking lot, I receive a text message from Zeke.

"Booking confirmed. Keeley will come to you @ 17:30. Reservation @ Motel 5 on Hollywood Blvd under Jessa Monroe. Text back when you have the room number."

I relay the information to Mary Sue, who rolls her eyes and responds, "Motel 5. Great. The hotel that makes Motel 6 look like the Ritz Carlton."

We make our way down to Hollywood and check into our reservation, using the petty cash we received from wardrobe to pay for the room. Inside, I can't help but take silent pleasure as I watch the motel clerk's internal struggle as he tries not to assume we are sex workers, but can't stop himself. People are such puppets.

By the time we get to our room, it's already almost 5:00. My, how time flies when you spend the day driving back and forth across L.A. and getting a complete head-to-toe make-over in the middle of it all.

I text our room number to Zeke, and Mary Sue settles onto the bed and turns on the T.V. while we wait. I can't settle for anything so mundane—I'm too hyped up, so instead I pace across the room, counting down the seconds until our mark arrives.

Every pore, every nerve in my body is tingling with anticipation. My oldest, dearest friend, Death, is just around the corner. Soon—oh, so soon—I will be taking the knife from my purse and plunging it deep, deep into soft, moist flesh. The tension of knowing a cathartic release is coming . . . I tell you, it's better than sex.

The fact it's a man who I'll be killing is just icing on the cake. I have always preferred killing men. Working for T.H.E.M. I usually don't get to be selective about who I kill, but before I was recruited all but one of the thirteen people I had killed were men. The woman was just me going through an experimental phase, really. Trying it out to see if I liked it. She was alright, I won't deny I still enjoyed it, but really there is nothing more satisfying in this world than killing a man. You can just call me Sarah the Heterogametic Slayer.

"Girlfriend, you're making *me* dizzy with all that pacing," Mary Sue snaps in an uncharacteristic display of irritation—normally it's my job to be the bitter one in our relationship.

Realizing that if I managed to get on Mary Sue's nerves, I must be in bad shape, I stop pacing and sit on the edge of the bed, my fingers twitching and my feet tapping with continued anticipation.

"Sorry," I respond to her, "I'm just revved up. I haven't killed anyone since . . . well, you know . . . Duluth . . . "

"Yeah, I know hon, but trust me—a watched corpse never croaks."

I can't help but laugh—Mary Sue always has a way with words.

"So, have you talked to Jason lately?" she asks, not-so-subtly.

Porcupines, sometimes I really hate this woman. She knows about Jason and me because she was training under Jason to become an *ass*assin around the time I broke up with him. For a while, I suspected Mary Sue may have been the woman he was cheating on me with (I never actually was able to *catch* him at it, but I knew he was seeing someone else). If I'm going to be honest, part of me *still* wonders, but even if Mary Sue is the one, that was before I knew her and Jason and I were long over and done with by the time she came into my life a few months ago.

But Mary Sue and Jason are still on speaking terms, and so every chance she gets she brings him up, no doubt trying to speak on his behalf. She claims she believes him when he says he never cheated on me, but I know what I know and I know the dirt bag is a cheating asshole. So there.

"Nope. And I'm not going to," I respond, as always.

"Mmkay," she says with a nonchalant shrug, then returns to watching TV. Her casual attitude about it all makes me want to scream and strangle her tiny, currently Asian neck. The only things stopping me are the facts that: 1) killing a co-worker would definitely count as voiding my T.H.E.M. contract, and 2) I'm pretty sure the calculating little twat intends to rile me up this way, and I'll be damned if I'm going to give her the satisfaction of knowing she got me angry enough to murder her.

Suddenly, my phone vibrates and I nearly jump through the ceiling into the room above us. I pick up my phone, and see a text from Zeke: "He is on his way up."

5

BARELY A FEW MINUTES later, a knock comes at the door. Mary Sue and I both straighten ourselves up, and then I head to the door.

"Gene?" I say in my sultriest voice as I crack open the door. Standing in the hall is a man in his late-forties to early-fifties. Thin, wiry frame complimented by wire-rimmed glasses. Hair gone completely grey. Not unhandsome, *per se*, but not Harrison Ford, either.

"Yes—Jessa? May I come in?" he asks—even if Zeke hadn't already told me as much, I can tell from the confidence in his voice that he is no stranger to the courtesan profession and this is most definitely not his first rodeo. It will, however, be his last.

"Of course, sugar," I respond, putting on a façade of seduction whilst I internally shrivel up in disgust.

I undo the door latch, and step aside so he can enter. A look of confusion spreads across his face when he sees Mary Sue—*Ming*—sitting on the bed.

"What's going on?" He asks, his voice betraying his concerns of being conned.

"She's in training," I respond, placing a hand calmingly on his chest. "You get two for the price of one."

"Me ruv you rong time," Mary Sue 'helpfully' adds to the conversation.

I strain a couple facial muscles resisting the urge to roll my eyes. Then, acting as if Mary Sue had not said anything at all, I ask, "That's not a problem is it?"

For a moment—a *brief* moment, mind you—suspicion lingers in his face, no doubt fearing he is about to be up-priced or caught in a police sting, but after looking back and forth between myself and Mary Sue a few times, his male-ness wins out over his suspicion and he replies, "No, no. No problem at all."

Pig.

He reaches into his pocket, pulls out an unmarked envelope, and 'discreetly' places it on the desk by the door. I nod at Mary Sue, who gets up and takes the envelope into the restroom to count Senator Keeley's 'donation.'

While she counts, I lead the senator toward the bed and help him relieve himself of his jacket, which I drape over the desk chair. He sits on the edge of the bed and I sit behind him, rubbing his shoulders, and ask, "So, what brings to you the City of Angels, handsome?"

"Oh . . . just in on business," he replies.

For a politician, he sure is a crappy liar, so it's probably just as well Mary Sue and I will be relieving him of his responsibilities shortly.

Mary Sue steps out of the bathroom and I give her an inquiring glance, to which she only nods in response. "Looks like we're good to go, sweetie," I say, as I slide out from behind him and let Mary Sue take my place, rubbing his neck, as I climb onto his lap, straddling him as I begin to kiss him—trying not to gag as he shoves his tongue practically down my throat. I distract myself by keeping my purse—and the knife within—in the sideline of my vision, just within my reach on the nightstand.

Mary Sue starts to kiss his neck, and the next thing I notice is his hand sliding up my thigh, under my dress. Every muscle in my body tenses with utter disgust, and then . . .

I honestly can't tell you what happened. I must have blacked out or something, because next thing I know I'm standing over the senator, breathing heavily, knife in hand, and absolutely drenched in his blood.

Mary Sue is still sitting on the bed behind the senator, her jaw hanging open slightly. "You could've at least let me have *some* of the fun," she says, though the tremor in her voice betrays the sarcastic quip really was just to cover up the fact that I have startled her— and I can tell you Mary Sue, despite her ditzy nature, is *not* easily startled.

I look down at the blood-soaked senator and suddenly realize he's not quite dead—yet. Blood bubbles out of the corner of his mouth as he sputters out his dying breaths.

Suddenly, his eyes glaze over—but it is not the glaze of death . . . no, this is something . . . different. Trust me, I've seen the 'glaze of death' enough times to be able to recognize it.

There is still consciousness in his eyes—probably more consciousness than there had been moments before—but now there's something of a distant, crazed glint to his glare. More intent, more focused. If I believed in Voodoo magic, the combination of this horrifying glare and his bloody visage would make me think he'd turned into a zombie.

"Sarah . . . " the senator rasps in an unearthly voice, sending an ice-cold chill into every bone in my body, "Nick . . . says . . . hi . . . "

And then, he is dead.

Mary Sue and I say no words—we both know what needs to be done. Mary Sue leaves to go buy me a new dress, as the one I am currently wearing is forever ruined with blood stains, and we'd like to be able to leave the motel and return to headquarters without being arrested.

While she is out, I retreat to the bathroom, peel off the bloody dress, and step into the shower. I turn up the water as hot as I can stand, but it does nothing to erase the chill that has penetrated every marrow of my body—and the senator's last words play an endless loop in my mind.

"Sarah . . . Nick . . . says . . . hi . . . "

With each repetition of the haunting loop, a fresh shiver of chills travels through my body.

I stay in the shower until the draining puddle of water at my feet no longer shows even the faintest hint of red, then turn the water off and step out into the frigid air of the bathroom. I wrap myself in a towel and crumple into a ball in a corner of the restroom—every nerve in my body trembling.

But I don't cry. I haven't cried in nearly fifteen years.

I stay that way for I don't know how long. Fifteen, thirty minutes. Hell, it could be an hour for all I know.

I'm snapped back to reality by the sound of the

motel room door opening, signaling Mary Sue's return. There is a knock on the bathroom door, and then it opens a crack, just enough for Mary Sue's hand to slip through, holding a brand new dress (one much more comfortable and less skimp than the one tainted with the ex-senator's blood).

I force myself to pull together, pick myself up off the floor, and cross the bathroom to take the proffered dress. Mary Sue's hand disappears, the door closes, and I pull the dress over my head. I look at myself in the mirror, and a stranger looks back at me—though not just because of my altered appearance.

The dress Mary Sue picked out is a flowery sundress—normally this would be *way* too girly for my tastes, but right now I couldn't care less about anything like that. All I want is to get out of this motel room and away from that fucking senator's corpse as soon as possible.

I wrap the blood-soaked dress in a towel and step out of the bathroom to find Mary Sue is already set to leave, both of our purses in hand. She opens up my purse for me to drop the towel with the ruined dress inside, and as I do so I see she had already retrieved the knife and put it inside the purse, as well.

We don't bother wiping down the room for fingerprints—one of the perks of being a T.H.E.M. agent is your fingerprints are automatically expunged from any and all police records.

We leave the room in silence and head out of the hotel lobby—the clerk probably confused by my change of wardrobe, but I don't give a rat's ass about that right now. It isn't until we are on the highway, headed back towards headquarters, that Mary Sue breaks the awkward silence and says, "What the *fuck* just happened?"

"Fucked if I know," I respond dryly. The severity of the situation is marked by the fact that Mary Sue does not offer her usual response of, "Then you better find out."

Instead, all she says is, "So, what do we do now?"

"Only one thing to do," I respond.

I pull out my phone and text Zeke, "Job is done. We need to speak. NOW. Face-to-face. It's about Nick."

Barely seconds have passed before I get an aggravating one-word response: "Fine."

6

VERY RARELY DOES Zeke grant an in-person audience, so the fact he accepted my request without question shows just how fucked up this whole Nick Jin situation is.

Mary Sue and I return to headquarters and make our way through the underground labyrinth to an office all the way at the back of the building—Zeke's office. I've barely raised my hand to knock on the door when I hear Zeke's slithery voice call out, "Come in." I don't know how the hell he does that, since there aren't any cameras in the hallway (at least none I've ever been able to pick out).

Mary Sue and I enter the office and close the door behind us. You might think the office of the leader of a super secret organization of trained serial killers would look like your stereotypical Bond villain evil lair. Sinister gadgets ticking mechanically in the background. Vials of chemicals bubbling with nefarious purpose. Instruments of torture hanging from the walls like a high schooler's swim meet trophies. A map of the world with various attack plans marked, detailing schemes of global domination. A large tank filled with laser-equipped sharks.

But alas. As is often the case, reality is far less romantic than fiction. Zeke's office looks like nothing more than your average CEO's office. A desk placed exactly at the center of the room, littered with an array of papers and to do lists. Filing cabinets in the corner. You'd think he'd at least go all out and get one of those massive, leather swivelly chairs so when you enter he could spin around, revealing himself petting a Persian cat, sipping brandy and say, "So. We meet again." But no. Just a boring old, black, standard office swivelly chair.

The only real difference between this office and any other CEO's office is the reports littering Zeke's desk and stored in his filing cabinets don't list productivity details and stocks analytics, but people that need to be murdered. It's one of those tiny details the Devil just loves to go on about.

And then, there's the man himself. It's been a few years since I've actually seen Zeke (like I said, he doesn't grant face-to-face meetings often, and it's not exactly like T.H.E.M. is the type of place to throw an annual picnic or Christmas Party . . .), and he is not looking good. Granted, he never looked good as far as I'm concerned, but worse than usual. He's lost a lot of weight—which *should* be a positive, but in Zeke's case it just makes him look ill and like his skin is too big for his body, as if he just simply picked out a suit that was a few sizes too large. His eyes look sunken and tired. He never was exactly the warmest of people I'd ever met, but there's an iciness in his stare now that tells me immediately to test his boundaries would not be wise for my health.

Mary Sue and I pull out two chairs at the desk

opposite from Zeke and sit down. "Talk," he commands.

I'm still in a state of shock, so I nod to Mary Sue to indicate for her to do the talking. "The job was going along fine, boss," she starts, "everything started off according to plan. Keeley showed up, we went through the routine of pretending to be escorts. We got his guard down and . . . and then we killed him, but as he was dying, he said–"

"He said, 'Sarah, Nick says hi,'" I finish for her, looking at the floor, my voice cold and dead.

Once again, I find myself in Mary Sue's debt, because I really don't want Zeke to know I had some sort of blackout and lost control. The last thing I need is for Zeke to bench me and force me to be evaluated. I think I'd go stir crazy, getting tested and having to wait on the side lines until I can go back in the field again.

Zeke remains silent for several moments, his leathery face unreadable as he takes this information in.

"That's all he said?" Zeke says at last, breaking the screaming silence.

"Yes," Mary Sue replies. "Maybe he was going to say more, I don't know. He died pretty much as soon as he said it."

"Did he . . . seem . . . *different*, when he said this?"

My eyes dart up from staring resolutely at the floor and bore into Zeke's. *How did he know?*

"Yes," I reply, unable to keep the tone of suspicion out of my voice. "It was like he . . . like . . . Porcupines, you know I don't believe in superstitious bullshit, Zeke, but it was like he'd become *possessed* or something . . .

41

it was like someone else was speaking through him . . . fuck, I know how that sounds, but that's what it was like."

"She's telling the truth," Mary Sue replied, taking my hand and giving it a reassuring squeeze. I resist my natural urge to smack her upside the head. I don't like people touching me, even (or especially) well-meaning people like Mary-fucking-Sue.

Zeke nods once, seemingly affirmed in some suspicion—though he offers no clarification—then he rises and begins pacing slowly behind his desk, deliberating.

"I'm not going to lie to you, two," he says at last. "The situation with Nick Jin is becoming more and more problematic. You may have been the first person he reached out to, Sarah, but you weren't the last. He has continued reaching out to our operatives, trying to recruit more to his cause, and I'm sorry to say not everyone he reached out to was as loyal as you were."

"Gee boss, should I reach into a raggedy hat and pull out a magical sword?" I retort, unable to help myself.

Zeke shoots me a warning glance, but otherwise ignores the interruption. "He's already recruited three P.S.K. agents and one assassin to his ranks, and he killed another P.S.K. who refused his offer. He's approached a few others who refused him and were able to fight him off, but none of them were able to apprehend him, either. It is clear he has a way of monitoring our activities, as he always knows when and where an agent has been put on assignment—though *how* he is obtaining this information, I can't say at this time."

This isn't really new or surprising information to me. In my dealings with Nick last fall, I had noticed that somehow he must have had some sort of surveillance technique on myself and/or T.H.E.M. He always seemed to be one step ahead of me and Mary Sue, and there were . . . *things* he knew about me that he shouldn't have been able to know. *Personal* things he was able to use and manipulate me. I still can't believe I actually fucked the fucker. I will *never* forgive myself for that (even if he *was* disguised to look like my favorite *Mr. What* star).

"So, what? You think he found out we were going to mark the senator and just 'gave him a message' to relay to me?" I ask, my voice incredulous.

"More or less, yes. The . . . uh . . . 'trance' you mentioned was probably just a result of Keeley being in the throes of death. That is the simplest explanation, after all."

I don't doubt Zeke is keeping his promise and telling us the truth—however, I would have to be a complete moron to believe he is telling us *everything* he knows, and I sure as fuck do not believe for a second that Keeley's 'trance' was just a dying man's insanity. But I know Zeke will *never* divulge information to me once he's decided I shouldn't know it, so I don't press the matter any further.

"Okay, fine. What do we do next?" Mary Sue asks— I can tell by her tone she's as convinced of Zeke's forthrightness as I am.

"Well, the way I see it, we have two options. Since it seems that for some reason Nick is singling you out, Sarah, either I take you out of service immediately and place you into T.H.E.M. protective custody until Nick is successfully apprehended, or we take a chance and place you on assignment immediately, in the hopes that it brings Nick and his defectors out of hiding—in essence, you will be our live bait. I have my thoughts on the matter, but I will leave the decision ultimately in your hands."

Once again, I am thankful Mary Sue omitted my blackout fugue attack on the senator. I'm pretty sure at this point if Zeke had that little nugget of information he would not be offering me this choice.

"Put me on assignment," I respond without a second's hesitation.

If I didn't know any better, I'd say I saw a momentary flash of pride in Zeke's eyes, but it must have been just a trick of the light. I have no reason to believe Zeke looks at me any differently, or with any more admiration, than any of the other P.S.K. agents in his employ.

"Very well. Go home and get some rest, both of you. I will contact you in the morning once I have selected an appropriate assignment for you."

"*Both of us*?" I repeat, hoping I misheard him. Mary Sue and I get on okay and all, at least compared to my other relationships with people, but even so I'd prefer not have to spend another several months trapped with her on assignment.

"You know the rules, Sarah. No one—especially not you, considering Nick is singling you out—goes on assignment alone. The fact that this assignment is a setup to try and capture Nick is just even more reason for you to have assistance. If you'd rather have–"

"Fine, fine," I say. I've already heard Jason's name one-and-a-half too many times today. I don't need to hear it again.

At that Zeke, dismisses us.

We return to the domain of the F.U.C.K.'s, and forty-five minutes later we are back to our normal selves. A quick trip to wardrobe to return our rented supplies (the purses and dresses—my dress of course will have to be incinerated, due to all of the 'evidence' staining it) and reclaim our personal clothing and belongings, and the assignment for Senator Keeley is officially done and closed.

As we make our way out of headquarters, there is much we need to talk about, but neither of us dares talking within the walls of T.H.E.M., for if any set of walls had ears, it would be the walls of those subterranean hallways. Mary Sue attempts to make small talk to fill the awkward silence, but I deplore small talk, and she eventually gives up.

Once outside in the parking lot, however, I feel a bit more comfortable talking openly.

"Do you believe any of what he said?" I ask, as we walk across the nearly empty lot toward our respective vehicles.

"I think what he said was true. What he *didn't* say, however, is a different matter," she responds cryptically. When all I do is nod sullenly, she continues, "It's a clusterfuck, but I think the only way for you and me to get more information and get to the bottom of all this is if Nick gets captured, so we might as well play our part and try to make that happen."

"I agree," I admit, though it leaves a hollow feeling in my gut—I still can't shake the creepy image of the senator becoming 'possessed' and croaking those haunting words at me with his last breaths.

"Chin up, short-stack," Mary Sue says, bopping me

under the chin lightly with her fist. *Her* calling *me* short-stack is rich, considering I'm at least a foot taller than her pipsqueak, Oompa-Loompa self. "Tomorrow the Terrible Two-Some of Sick and Misk will be back on the case, killin' hoes and mo-fos in their sleep. The Killer Sisters are back, girlfriend!"

Despite myself, I smile and return Mary Sue's proffered high-five. No matter how much I try, I never seem able to hate her for very long.

7

NEEDLESS TO SAY, rest does not come easy to me. I spend most of the night fitfully tossing and turning. In the few moments I do manage to doze off, I'm woken by nightmares of a zombie Senator Keeley strangling me and moaning in a repeated chant, "Nick says hi . . . Nick says hi . . . "

So by the time Zeke calls me at 6:00 in the morning (the sadistic bastard loves calling me early, because he knows I'm not a morning person), I feel like I would have been better off not even trying to sleep.

"Good morning star shine, the Earth says hello!" Zeke says. I'm so tired, it takes me a minute to figure out who he's impersonating this time. Then it hits me, and I literally face-palm. Willy Wonka— and not the Gene Wilder Willy, but the Johnny Depp Willy. Technically not a serial killer, but definitely a sociopath, and I guess after thirty or forty years of doing this, Zeke's probably running out of good characters to impersonate.

"Cut the crap, Zeke, I'm in no mood today," I snap.

"Sounds like someone's having a case of the Mondays," Zeke replies, but gets down to business. "I have you on a three-way with Misk so I don't have to repeat myself."

"You *wish* you had us on a three-way, Zeke," Mary Sue replies, and I can just picture the sarcastic glint in her eye.

"Your loss. Anyway, I have your assignment picked out and ready. I'm sending you to Tennessee."

"For fuck's sake Zeke . . . are you *trying* to punish me?" I snap. He knows I don't handle myself well in the south. Bible Belters and I for some reason just don't get along. Okay, okay. *Most people* and I don't get along, but sanctimonious types and me really don't gel very well. Probably has something to do with my being a sociopathic serial killer and all. Kinda rubs against their whole 'Thou shalt not kill' thing they like to harp on about.

"How about you hear the assignment before you bite my head off, sweetheart?" Zeke snaps. I know I've crossed a line, so I zip it and let him proceed. "I chose this one for you because it will be a quick job. No more than a month or two at the most. We want this to be a quick job, for a few reasons. For one, it will tell us for certain if Nick really is singling you out, or if you just happened to piss him off by defying him last October. If he's just a little ticked, then he probably wouldn't waste his time and resources following you on such a short assignment. But if he does have a personal vendetta against you, for whatever reason, then he will probably follow you wherever I send you. And if that *is* the case, then I want you to be able to get the assignment finished quickly before he has a chance to fuck it up like he almost did in Minnesota."

"Makes sense to me, boss," Mary Sue chirps in. Ass-kisser as always. "What are the details?"

"There's a family in Bucksnort—"

"*Bucksnort?*" I repeat, cutting him off with a derisive snort. "Why don't you just send us to Toadspawn or Heehawville?"

Zeke clears his throat with irritation, but otherwise ignores my interruption. "There's a family in Bucksnort who the governor of Tennessee has reason to believe are leading a local K.K.K. uprising. He wants them 'taken care of' before the story gets out and makes national headlines.

"Obviously we can't station you immediately in Bucksnort—the town's too small and the project's too short, there's no way to make your presence inconspicuous. So, we will be setting you up at a hotel in Dickson—about an hour from Nashville, and a half hour from Bucksnort."

I have to keep myself from snorting every time Zeke says the name 'Bucksnort.'

"The governor doesn't give a flying fuck about how you get rid of the family," Zeke continues, "just as long as you keep the Klan out of it. He's trying to save face—and hopefully prevent retaliation riots and more lives lost."

"So I guess we shouldn't go in as black women fighting against white supremacy?" Mary Sue asks.

"That would not be advised," Zeke replies in a monotone drone. Despite the bland tone of his reply, I can't help but detect a slight hint of amusement coming over the line.

"What's our cover?" I ask.

"Up to you. Basically just keep a low profile. We're putting you up in a five star hotel—we're going with the assumption that at a higher-end establishment they won't ask too many questions and they won't be likely to link any of their guests to a crime committed half an hour away. Just stay under the radar and don't trash the room or have any of your wild swinging orgy parties. The governor would probably not appreciate that very much."

"Damnit, Zeke, you take all of the fun out of everything," Mary Sue quips.

"It's what I do. We aren't going to waste any time on this—your flight leaves tonight at 17:15. Misk, a town car will be arriving at your apartment in half an hour. Sick, it will then stop by to pick you up and bring you both here to headquarters. As soon as you're done with the Makeover Specialists and wardrobe, it will take to you L.A.X. Sick, do you have any problems with this arrangement?"

Mary Sue must be confused as fuck, but I know why he's singling me out. This schedule will prevent me from paying my usual pre-assignment visit to my mother in prison. You might think it's sweet of him to make sure I'm okay with not being able to visit my mother before I go on assignment, but I know better. This has nothing to do with him being concerned about my well-being or happiness, and everything to do with reminding me I am nothing but his bitch on a leash. After all, it's not *that* big of a deal if I don't visit her before I go on a mission. It's not like she's expecting me or anything. I'll just visit her when I get back, so the *only* reason for him to bring this up is to get under my skin—and as always it works. I really hate how this man is able to play me like a mother-fucking fiddle.

He just can't come out and say anything directly about my mother on the line because he knows Mary

Sue is listening. For *that* at least, I am thankful. The last thing I will *ever* need is to have to get into a girly heart-to-heart about my mother with Mary Sue.

"No Zeke, I am have no problem," I reply curtly, placing as much frost and ice as I can muster into each syllable.

"Good. Do either of you have any questions for me before we wrap up this conversation?"

"Just one for you, Easy—are you going to be suing Jenny Craig, because you looked like shit last night," I snap, still bitter over his insinuations about my mother. 'Easy' by the way is a pet name I have for Zeke, and it's about the only weapon I have that seems to be able to actually get under *his* skin. I use it sparingly, so it doesn't lose its effect, and save it for moments when he has particularly irked me (and yes, most of those moments are spawned by him insinuating about my mother).

"Fuck you, too, Sick," he responds with deadly calm in his voice. "If that's all, you two had better get ready for your rides."

And with that, the line goes dead.

Even though I'm pressed for time, I allow myself the guilty pleasure of mutilating another victim from my cabinet of cuddly curiosities. That's two fluffy casualties in barely twenty-four hours. As the innards of the teddy bear fly across my room, I reflect that I'm going to have to make a stop at a Toys 'R' Us while I'm in Tennessee. I then remember I will be sharing this assignment with Mary Sue, and will therefore definitely be needing some extra fluffy victims. I really should have bought stock in Toys 'R' Us *years* ago . . .

8

AN HOUR LATER, Mary Sue and I are in a town car being escorted to headquarters. We are both so exhausted even Mary Sue takes the ride in silence—which is not a natural state of being for her.

I get a strange sense of *déjà vu* as—for the second time in twenty-four hours—we make our way through the porn warehouse to the secret entrance to the subterranean corridors, and back to the domain of the F.U.C.K.'s.

"See ya in a few, girlfriend!" Mary Sue chirps cheekily, the first words she's uttered all morning, as we separate into our respective make-over rooms.

I groan audibly when I see that, unlike yesterday, my team of F.U.C.K.'s are all men. I guess they decided to even it out and let Mary Sue have a turn with . . . what was her name? Jenny? Gemma? Geranium? Meh, whatever. Not like it matters.

"Please take it easy on the boobs this time, guys," I sigh resignedly, and with little hope of being listened to.

Sure enough, all I get in response is a smirk from the lead F.U.C.K., a pimply, freckled, bespectacled, ginger kid who looks like he couldn't be barely out of high school, and probably the only boobs he has seen other than in a smut rag are from working at this job. This is not going to end well for me, I fear.

I try to zone out during the procedure, but that's really hard to do when you're getting poked, prodded, and stabbed all over your body incessantly. Maybe it's just because yesterday's session was a quick job, but it seems like it takes twice as long as usual today. In actuality, however, after the F.U.C.K.'s are done and I dip into the bubbling water of the hot tub, I look at the clock on the wall and see only the standard six hours have passed. Time flies when you're being poked and prodded by obnoxious horny dweebs. And, just as I had suspected, I can't help but notice my boobs have at least doubled in size. Fucking F.U.C.K.'s.

An hour later, I regretfully pull myself out of the soothing bubbles, pull on a robe, and meet Mary Sue in the hallway to make our way down to wardrobe. Sure enough, I can tell Mary Sue had . . . whatever-her-name-is on her team, just by the sheer absence of a noticeable boob job. It takes me most of the walk to wardrobe to adjust to my new weight distribution. Fucking F.U.C.K.'s.

Mary Sue more or less looks like she did the first time I met her—blonde and blue-eyed, but smaller in the chest area. There are still enough differences that you probably wouldn't recognize her as 'Bethany' (the dupe identity she went as on our assignment in Minnesota) unless you looked really closely, but I actually find it comforting to have her be moderately familiar to me. After we came back from Minnesota, I never really was able to reconcile the 'real' brunette, kinda-nerdy-looking Mary Sue with the blonde bimbo I'd come to know while on assignment.

Unlike yesterday, we don't get to browse through T.H.E.M.'s underground Ross Warehouse, as wardrobe has already set aside four suitcases (two for each of us) of clothes, passports, etc. We each take our designated suitcases and step into our private dressing rooms. I drop my robe to the floor and survey my new self in the dressing room mirror.

Aside from the over-zealous boob job, I'm not too disappointed. I've definitely suffered worse at the hands of the F.U.C.K.'s (on my last trip to Minnesota, they went out of their way to make me look like Jessica-Fucking-Rabbit). My hair has turned from dark brown to dirty blonde. My green eyes are a dark, enchanting shade of blue. Whereas yesterday they made me paler, today they've given me a slightly darker complexion and a set of freckles that would turn Jennifer Lawrence green with envy (in fact, I note I bear a slight resemblance to J. Law, if she were to get a massive boob job, that is).

I browse through the first suitcase, and since I'll be flying tonight in a few hours, opt to go for a more comfortable travel ensemble—a pair of blue jeans, white tennis shoes, and a light-purple blouse. In the second suitcase, on top of a second set of clothes, I find a wallet with credit cards and cash, and my new passport (Zeke never lets me have a fake driver's license on assignment—he can't stop me from driving illegally when I'm not working, but he refuses to enable me when I'm on assignment if he can help it). My dupe name for the next month or so is going to be Nanetta Dieterle (I often wonder where the *fuck* they come up with these names . . .)

I close up my suitcases and step out of the dressing

room, and a few minutes later Mary Sue emerges, also.

"Well, hi there, nice to meet you," she says in one of the thickest southern drawls I have ever heard. "I'm Lindsay Buchanan. And you are?"

Of course. Not only did she avoid the annoying boob job, but she also got a perfectly normal name. Bitch.

Deciding I might as well follow her lead and get into character now, I respond (in a slightly less-obnoxious southern accent), "Hiya Lindsay, I'm Nanetta Dieterle. It sure is a pleasure to meet you."

This is the part I dislike most about the job—having to pretend to be another person. As a general rule, I hate other people, so chances are whatever persona I adopt for any given assignment, I am going to hate that person, and having to pretend to be someone you hate is really, really annoying. But there aren't many other jobs out there that pay you to kill large numbers of people on a regular basis, so I put up with the thespian bullshit and deal.

Our cheesy introduction completed, we return topside and get back into the town car, which is waiting patiently to take us to the airport.

On the drive, we put up the soundproof partition between us and the driver so we can discuss the assignment in private—this will probably be the last opportunity we have to talk without prying ears until we arrive at our hotel in Tennessee.

"So, just in case anyone at the hotel asks, what do you think our cover story should be?" Mary Sue asks, maintaining her southern accent. Even though we are essentially alone, it's always best to stay in character as much as possible, so we will be less likely to slip up when we *aren't* alone.

"I've been thinking about that," I respond. "We'll be there for at least a month, so we can't say we're just travelling on vacation or in town for a convention or anything. That won't fly. But we also won't be there for more than two-months, so our usual long-term cover stories won't work, either. We could say we're in town to deal with a death of a family member or something—but that might lead to questions we can't answer. I know Dickson ain't a small town where everyone knows everyone, but it's still not worth the risk. I'm thinking probably the easiest thing to say is we're there for work—legal assistants, or something like that, on a long-term project."

"I like the legal assistant idea," Mary Sue chips in. "It gives us a valid reason not to be able to answer any questions about what we're there for."

"Exactly." I don't mention this excuse came to me easily, as it's the same story I tell my mother about why I have to go out of town so often.

We discuss a few smaller details about our cover story—just to be prepared—but really we won't have too much more information about the case to talk about until we arrive in Tennessee and receive our case files (which will be waiting for us in our hotel rooms). We also agree to try and figure out some way to keep up my daily martial arts training—though we admit this will probably be difficult to find a way to do it discreetly.

The rest of the ride is pretty much spent with me tuning out Mary Sue's inane babbling (clearly, she is more awake now than she was this morning . . . I

wonder if the F.U.C.K.'s gave her a caffeine injection
. . .). As usual, she doesn't seem to mind or even notice
that I'm not paying her any attention.

My mind is still whirling around the events of the
last twenty-four hours. What did Nick do to Senator
Keeley that made him turn into that weird trance
state? Because I sure as hell don't believe Zeke's excuse
that he was just 'delivering a message' Nick gave him.
It's something weirder than that, I know it. I also think
back to something Nick said to me in Minnesota—
something about how I have no idea the things
T.H.E.M. are up to. That confused me at the time,
because what could he possibly think T.H.E.M. is up
to that would bother me, considering I already
obviously know they primarily focus on killing large
groups of people for hire. I mean, you can't really get
much shadier or scandalous than that, can you?

At the back of my mind, I can't shake the suspicion
that somehow these mysterious plots alluded to are
related somehow to the senator's trance, and Nick's
irritating surveillance methods that enable him to
know every movement T.H.E.M. is going to make,
practically before they've even made it (that, and his
really irritating ability to know things about me that
no one should know).

9

WE TOUCHDOWN IN Nashville at about 9:30 p.m. The flight was relatively uneventful, except for Mary Sue's incessant spew of verbal vomit. Being confined in a sardine can with this woman for four hours makes me want to suggest that Guantanamo Bay look into utilizing Mary Sue as a replacement method of torture as opposed to water boarding—half an hour into the flight and I was already at the point where I would tell anyone my deepest darkest secrets just for the sake of shutting her up.

By the time we landed however, we were both so exhausted after the long two days we just went through that Mary Sue is back to her previous, albeit non-characteristic, complacent and silent state. It's just as well that T.H.E.M. traditionally arranges transportation service for agents from the airport to their living arrangement, because I don't think either of us are in a state where we can be trusted to operate a motor vehicle (anyone who points out that my radar intolerance makes me permanently untrustworthy behind the wheel of a motor vehicle gets bitch-slapped right out of the pages of this book. You have been warned).

After we retrieve our luggage from the baggage claim, we find our chauffer waiting outside on the curb with a sign. At first the driver tries to make small talk with us as we pull out of the airport and onto the highway, but when even Mary Sue shows no interest in conversation, he gives up and puts up the divider between our cabin and the front of the town car.

Either time flies faster in Tennessee (and in my experience, it's the *opposite* that's true), or I must have dozed off at some point during the drive to Dickson, because it certainly does not feel like it has been forty-five minutes when we pull up under the entry awning of The Hotel Dickson.

Usually when on assignment, T.H.E.M. puts its agents up in an apartment for the duration of the assignment, due to the fact that our assignments usually last around six months or so, and a hotel stay for such a long period of time would raise eyebrows—not to mention we are usually trying to place ourselves as normal members of a community, so in order to achieve that effect we have to actually *live* in the community as a normal resident. As such, getting to stay in a hotel is something of a luxury—and my first impression of The Hotel Dickson is this is going to be one swanky luxury, to boot. The entryway automatic doors are gilded with gold. A thoroughly disgusting amount of crystal chandeliers, that would make the Phantom of the Opera start giggling with malicious glee, hang from the ceiling of the lobby. Hell, I wouldn't be surprised if the toilet seats are gold-plated. This is honestly the kind of hotel I'd expect to find overlooking Central Park in New York City, not in the middle of hoe-down Tennessee.

We have to wait to check-in, because a little old man who looks as if he might be keeling over any second is ahead of us, and there is only one desk clerk at this time of the night. The old man's check-in takes forever, because he apparently has to ask every single question possible about the hotel *right now*. "What time is breakfast served?" "What time does room service close?" "What time will checkout be?" "If I need to extend my reservation, is that a problem?" "If I decide to come back another time, are you pet friendly?" Honestly, I'm surprised the codger didn't ask where the nearest depends dispensary is located.

I can see the look of hope in the desk clerk's eye as he gets to the end of the check-in process, and of course Mr. Fuddy-Duddy insists on paying for his room up front with cash—despite being advised by the clerk that there will be an additional security deposit of one hundred dollars per night if he pays cash up front. The old man insists he always pays cash because he doesn't trust banks. Naturally, he has to count out each ten dollar bill individually and meticulously before handing the sum to the exhausted desk clerk. Hell, at this point, I'm just glad the old codger isn't paying with quarters.

Finally, the desk clerk asks, "Is there anything else I can help you with, Mr. Jorra?" and the old dude replies, "No, I guess that's all. Thank you, you've been very helpful. If I think of anything else, I will give you a call."

The words 'please don't' are practically scratched across the poor desk clerk's face.

At long last, it is our turn and we check in using credit cards provided by T.H.E.M., and I smile to see how relieved the desk clerk is over the ease of our check in. An over-nervous, twenty-something and pimply bellman named Tim assists us with our suitcases to our rooms on the twelfth floor. As we step off the elevator, Mr. Jorra—the codger who checked in before us—pushes into the elevator after us, looking a tad put out.

"I can't be this high," he mumbles at us, regardless of whether we are paying attention, "I told them when I made the reservation I need to be on a low floor because I have vertigo. They never listen."

I'm pretty sure he continued mumbling, but fortunately for us the closing of the elevator doors muted his tirade.

Tim the Bellman gives us a nervous, apologetic grimace, and then leads us to our rooms, which are right next to each other. On the one hand, part of me wants to be as far away from Mary Sue as possible for the sake of my sanity, but even I must admit it will be easier to plot and scheme inconspicuously if our rooms are closer. The sacrifices I make for work, sometimes . . .

Tim deposits our suitcases into our respective rooms and Mary Sue tips him well for his trouble and—just for the sake of seeing him squirm uncomfortably—gives him a peck on the cheek. As he turns as red as the monkey suit uniform he is wearing, Tim scuttles his way back to the elevator.

Once we hear the ding of the elevator door closing behind Tim the Bellman, Mary Sue turns to me and says, "Wait until morning to discuss the case?"

"Absolutely," I respond eagerly, for I certainly do not have the energy or brainpower to even try and think about our case at this point. "Maybe even a trip to the hotel spa will be in order first . . . "

"Now Nanetta," she admonishes, using my temporary assignment name just in case anyone happens to overhear us, "we're here for work, not play."

"Oh, come off it, Lindsay," I snap back. "We might as well enjoy ourselves as well—when we can."

Mary Sue rolls her eyes in mock resignation, but says, "Alright, alright. But *after* the spa we get down to business."

"Fair enough. G'night, Lindsay."

"Sleep well, Buttercup."

Once inside the privacy of my room, I use my last remaining energy to strip off my clothes—I'm too tired to even open up my suitcase to look for any nightwear, and so I collapse into a useless, naked heap onto my bed, on top of the covers and all. Within minutes I am asleep.

But it is not a restful sleep, for I'm haunted by disturbing dreams . . .

I'm back at my apartment in Los Angeles, and Jason is there. Apparently, this is taking place before we broke up, because we are making out pretty heavily—and while the subconscious me is recoiling at the activity, the *dream* me is definitely responding positively to Jason's advances. I don't know if this is a normal dream experience to be simultaneously split between your actual self and your dream self, but this is a first for me.

In the dream, my Dream-self closes her eyes, losing herself in the moment, but when she opens them, it is no longer Jason she is with but Nick—well, to be accurate, Nick in his David Brennan look-alike disguise (the same disguise he used to seduce me back in Minnesota).

The Subconscious-Me wants to jump into the dream-world so that I can scream and slap some sense into the Dream-Me. But I can't, and Dream-Me—unaware of Subconscious-Me's protestations—does not recoil from the sudden change of romantic partner, but if anything responds with even more fervor. I *really* hate Dream-Me.

Suddenly, Nick/David and Dream-Me are both naked—even though moments before we had definitely been clothed. Despite myself, Subconscious-Me can't help but note how much detail the dream has—Nick/David looks exactly as I remember him, down to the last gorgeous freckle. I've never had a dream be so . . . *detailed*. They've always been much more 'impressionistic' for me in the past.

With the advent of our sudden nakedness, the tension in the dream naturally intensifies ten-fold—both the arousal of Dream-Me and the horrified disgust of Subconscious-Me. When he enters Dream-Me, Subconscious-Me feels everything, too. It is as if I am trapped in a body that is not my own, able to feel everything happening to it, but unable to have any effect on what is happening. It is like I am being made love to and raped at the exact same time.

Just as the dream builds towards a climax—and by this point even Subconscious-Me would welcome the release, for no other reason than to have the simultaneous double feature horror/romance at last be over—the dream shifts again, and I am back at the start of the dream with Jason, fully clothed and just in the early stages of make-out arousal. Dream-Me seems to be completely unaware of the change, but Subconscious-Me is fully aware and infuriated.

This infuriating loop repeats through my subconscious mind for the rest of the night, so when I finally awake the next morning I am thoroughly frustrated, in every way possible. A trip to the hotel's spa is more warranted than ever, but unfortunately when I look at the hotel's welcome booklet, I see the spa won't be open for another hour. I. Could. *Scream*.

I call the hotel operator to make an appointment at the spa so I can be sure to get in as early as possible, and then I decide to kill the extra hour taking a bath, and am pleased to find my luxury suite comes fully equipped with Jacuzzi. I take full advantage of the jets to relieve much of the tension pent up from my night of unresolved sex dreams. Only because he's the lesser of the two evils that were haunting my subconscious all night, I focus my thoughts on Jason instead of Nick/David and am—on some level—irritated to find that thinking of Jason like this for the first time in years does not bother me anymore. I blame Nick for this unforgiveable change of feeling. How *dare* he turn my ex into a relatively acceptable fantasy object. I swear, for the millionth time since Minnesota, if I ever run into Nick Jin again, I am going to murder the bastard slowly and with much delight.

My carnal frustrations *finally* appeased, I allow myself to float for several minutes in Jacuzzi bubbles and afterglow before climbing out of the bath, drying myself off, and getting dressed for my spa appointment. I still have a few minutes left to spare before my appointment, so I grab a quick breakfast from the hotel restaurant, and then make my way to the spa.

I spend twenty minutes steaming in the sauna, and

then to the massage parlor to meet my masseuse—a disgustingly attractive and well-built guy named Bill. If I hadn't *already* taken care of that element of my frustrations, I might have been tempted to invite Bill up to my room for a more thorough rub-down, however that would be a bad idea. Not because I'm on assignment—T.H.E.M. has zero policy about 'fraternizing' while on assignment. It's just I have this unfortunate tendency of wanting to kill men after I sleep with them (it's how I earned the nickname the Preying Mantis from the feds before T.H.E.M. recruited me). Jason was the only exception to that rule. Fucking bastard. So in summary, it's just as well I took care of *that* by myself.

Half an hour later, my massage done, I finally feel like I will be able to focus on the task at hand, so I return to my room to find Mary Sue waiting impatiently in the hallway, her right foot tapping and her case file tucked under her arm.

"Where *have* you been, Nanetta?" she asks, irritably.

"You can go fuck yourself," I reply curtly. "I told you I needed a trip to the spa first."

"Fine, whatever," she replies, rolling her eyes, but I know her well enough to suspect her irritation is only surface-level. It takes a lot to *actually* irritate Mary Sue. "Let's get on with this, shall we?"

I agree without complaint, and we enter my room to set to work.

10

CROSS THE room to my bed and kneel down by the safe under the bedside cabinet. I open the safe with a combination provided to me in my T.H.E.M. documentation and pull out a stack of manila envelopes—my case files. The safe, of course, had been sent by T.H.E.M. to the hotel to be placed in my room prior to arrival, and a duplicate safe is in Mary Sue's room, as well.

"You haven't even looked at those yet, have you," Mary Sue tisks with annoyance, indicating the envelopes in my hands.

I roll my eyes, then retort, "For the love of Captain Hammer's nipples, Lindsay, gimme a break already." Even though we are now in the privacy of my suite, it's probably best to stay in character, just in case a housekeeper walks in on us or something, and so I maintain my accent and use of Mary Sue's dupe name.

"Fine, whatever," Mary Sue huffs in annoyance. "While you're *catching up*, I'm gonna order room service. Do you want anything?"

"No, I already ate," I say as I plop myself onto my bed and start opening the case files. After a short beat, I remember to add, "Thank you."

While Mary Sue orders, I start sifting through the case files—a series of photographs and pages of data about the family we'll be targeting—the Andersons. Head of the family is Don Anderson, aged forty-six, professional mechanic. Looking at his photo, I note a passing resemblance to the mayor from *Jaws*. Then there's Don's younger brother Charlie, a forty-four year-old truck driver, and brother-in-law Clark Grobe, the latter married to the youngest Anderson sibling, Becky Grobe, thirty-eight. According to the documents, Clark is unemployed living off welfare and Becky works full time as a diner waitress to pay the rest of their bills. Don Anderson is currently married to his third wife, Virginia, and Charlie Anderson is still on his first marriage, Linda Buckwidth-Anderson.

Between the three families, there are twelve cousins in the younger generation, ages ranging from twelve (Timothy, Clark and Becky's youngest) to twenty-eight (Lorena, Don's oldest from his first marriage). Seven boys, five girls. Don, across his three marriages, has the largest group of kids—six—while Charlie and Linda have four and Clark and Becky reign in at only two.

Now, before you get your panties all bunched up, don't worry about the kids. T.H.E.M. does not target innocent young. Even a sinister organization of mass murderers has to draw the line somewhere. Of course, the definition of 'innocence' is a bit murky, so as a general rule we draw the line at high school. For this project in particular, our primary concern will be focusing on the members who are partaking in the family's 'extra-curricular activities,' so the younger kids will be safe, anyway.

Moving along, Don Anderson has a long history of White Supremacist activities, despite never officially being linked to the K.K.K. Numerous arrests for assault on various people of color, starting at the age of seventeen, some citations for disorderly conduct, etcetera. According to the Governor's personal statement, they believe Don Anderson joined the local K.K.K. group shortly after dropping out of high school in his senior year, and gradually rose throughout the ranks over the years until becoming the local leader within the last five years.

Up until recently, the Governor did not see the family and their supporters as a viable threat. Nobody paid much attention to the K.K.K. anymore, they were believed to be an ineffective splinter group of bitter old white guys still angry about the result of the Civil War. Everyone knew they were there and around, but nobody took them seriously—just like the creepy uncle who you have to endure some awkward remarks and inappropriate gestures from at family reunions, but can safely put out of your mind the rest of the time.

But, recently, with the growing rise of hate groups, The Powers That Be no longer can afford to put 'Creepy Uncle Bill' out of their minds. And so here we are, Mary Sue and I, in a fancy hotel room in Tennessee, researching this one family of 'Creepy Uncle Bills' for the sake of saving the governor and his state from national public embarrassment before they succeed at causing any mischief.

According to the governor's intel, Charlie and Clark both are also involved with brother Don's efforts, as well as the four boys that are over eighteen: John, Duke, Clark Jr., and Bobby—John and Duke being the sons of Papa Don, Clark Jr. being the Grobes' older boy, and Bobby being the oldest boy of Charlie and Linda. The women of course, according to standard White Supremacy tradition, stay home and do the cleaning while the men put on their big boy pants and do their manly things. On the plus side, at least this means the young children won't be completely orphaned . . .

Will it surprise you to learn that I am *greatly* looking forward to killing these despicable examples of human excrement?

"So, what do you think?" Mary Sue asks, sitting down on the bed next to me. I'd become so engrossed in reading the files, I hadn't even noticed that her food had been delivered and devoured.

"I'm thinking I'm going to enjoy killing these douche bags so much, it's almost wrong for me to get paid for it—*almost.*"

Mary Sue smirks, relaxing for the first time that morning. Clearly she just had a case of being hangry. "Yeah, that's for sure. But how do you think we should proceed?"

I ponder her question for a few moments, reminding myself she was trained as an *ass*assin, not a P.S.K., so she's not necessarily as versed at thinking through a P.S.K. assignment like I am.

"Well, we should start off with surveillance," I proceed after deliberating. "Spend two-to-three weeks, maybe more if necessary, watching the family, getting a sense of their routine. Once we're comfortable, move in for the kill."

"Are you thinking kill them all at once, or one by one?"

"That will largely depend on our surveillance, but I think in this instance all at once will be easier. Usually, for P.S.K. jobs we want to spread the killings out to make it more like a legit serial killer. But for this job, there's a lot more at stake. For example, once the family realizes they are being targeted, the rest might flee. We don't want that, so the best thing to do will be to do it quickly all at once—a spree killing, instead of a serial killing."

"What about our Herring, then? Will we just skip over creating a Herring persona?"

I smirk. Here you can tell the biggest difference between a P.S.K. and an *ass*assin. Mary Sue is perfectly content to kill her marks and just disappear into the night, no cover story to hide her tracks. Whereas I *love* the challenge of coming up with a cover story and can't imagine doing a job without one (even though on some level I admit it would make things easier).

"No," I respond at last after considering her question, "I think we should still have a Herring, if for no other reason than we don't want this to come back and bite the governor. If we leave the killings completely open-ended, conspiracy theorists might jump on it and say the family was killed by the government for their involvement in the K.K.K.—the fact that the conspiracy theorists would be *right*, for once, is beside the point. It's safer if we have a Herring in place."

All of that is true, but really my primary motivation to fight for this is the aforementioned fact that I like creating Herrings. Call me self-serving, if you must. You'd be right. Besides, if Zeke wanted this to be an *ass*assin job, he would have assigned it to an *ass*assin, not a P.S.K. So there.

"Okay, so what *will* our Herring be, then?" Mary Sue presses on, clearly disappointed I was able to out-reason her in this instance.

"Well, the easiest would be anti-hate retaliation," I respond, "but Zeke already told us we can't go that route. We will most likely need to wait until we've completed our surveillance to decide this for sure—pick out someone from the community to frame for the murders, someone who has a grudge or something against the Andersons. Shouldn't be too hard—in my experience, people who let hate rule their lives tend to have a lot of enemies. As a back-up plan, just in case we can't find anyone to frame, we can try to make it look like a trucker passing-through went yonkers and decided to role play *Wrong Turn*. But that would get complicated, so let's hope the family has an enemy we can believably frame."

"Alright. Fair enough. And what about our . . . *other* project?"

Ah yes. Nick. Despite my frustrating dream sequence of the night before, I had almost been able to forget about Nick.

"Well, main thing will be to keep an eye on the papers," I respond. "See if any unexplained killings start to happen. Last time, he sent me a coded message with the killings he'd made, so if that *does* start up again, let's also keep an eye out for any patterns so maybe we can get ahead of him that way. Also keep an eye out for any suspicious 'newcomers' to the area—anyone who, like us, has only just showed up in town. We already know he has a pretty decent ability to make himself over without the help of the F.U.C.K.'s—"

"The who?" Mary Sue asks, confused.

"Sorry. That's what I call T.H.E.M.'s make-over specialists. Stands for 'Fabricating Ugly Cock-Kissers.'"

"I like it. Filthy, but strangely appropriate," Mary Sue responds with a nod of approval.

"Anyway, he did a pretty decent job of making himself into a David Brennan lookalike–"

"He is *so* dreamy," Mary Sue interrupts, in a typical display of disgusting cheerleader girlyness. Yuck. "Definitely the best of the Misters. It was so sad when he left the show."

"I'm sure," refusing to admit out loud that I agree with her one-hundred percent on the matter. I may be a nerd, but I'm a closeted nerd and I'm okay with being closeted, so shut up. It's my life and if I want to stay in the closet about being a *Mister What* nerd, that's my prerogative.

"Anyway," I continue, getting back on track, "the point being, we don't know *who* or *what* Nick could be looking like, so we need to keep our guards up. We also need to remember, he has succeeded at recruiting other T.H.E.M. operatives to help him, so who knows how many people we could be up against."

"Fair enough," Mary Sue replies, straightening herself up, all business. "So what's our first move?"

"Our first move, Lindsay, is to drive over to Bucksnort—porcupines, I'm never going to be able to say that name with a straight face . . . anyway, we need to get over to Bucksnort and start our surveillance of the Anderson family."

Mary Sue smiles a devilish grin, reaches into one of her manila envelopes, and pulls out a set of car keys, "I'll drive."

11

BEFORE LEAVING, we each lock our case files back up in our respective safes, to keep the housekeepers from randomly stumbling upon them.

It is standard operating procedure for T.H.E.M. to have operatives use a company-issued vehicle while on assignment. As I've already explained, I'm something of an exception to that rule thanks to my radar sensitivity, which is one of the *few* advantages to being forced to have Mary Sue along with me on this assignment. I don't particularly enjoy being escorted around, but it's definitely preferable to having to take public transportation.

However, something—a mischievous glint in her eye, a slight smirk, an almost too-eager spring in her step—about Mary Sue's attitude as we make our way down to the hotel lobby makes me suspect she is hiding something, and I suspect that something has to do with our mode of transportation. By the time we get out of the hotel and into the parking lot, she is practically bursting at the seams with bubbly excitement, and it's enough to make me want to scream.

"Wait 'til you see this, Sare-bear," she says as we

approach a standard-looking, unassuming red Honda Civic (I cringe at the implementation of this new pet name for me . . . I don't like pet names . . .). "This is the latest innovation from the tech department. I knew they'd be rolling them out soon, but I didn't know we would have one on this assignment until I opened my case files this morning."

"Will you quit babbling and just show me already," I snap, in no mood for melodramatic theatrics this morning.

"Fine, fine, Miss Grumpy-pants," Mary Sue responds shortly. I decide not to point out that barely an hour ago *she* was the one being 'Miss Grumpy-pants.'

"Just watch this," and Mary Sue holds up the clicker attached to the car key, takes a quick glance around the parking lot to make sure we are alone, and then pushes a button on the clicker.

For a few seconds, nothing happens and I start to think Mary Sue was just pulling my leg, but then, before my eyes, I watch in amazement as the car changes from ruby red to sapphire blue.

"Ain't that nifty?" Mary Sue squeals with sheer elation. "The paint is a special blend which changes color when a certain electrical current is sent through it—kinda like those *Hot Wheels* toy cars that changed color when you put them in water."

"Nifty," I agree, definitely impressed.

"But that's not all," Mary Sue says with the air of a game show host about to reveal the next line of prizes, "check out this feature."

She pushes another button on the clicker, and with a whir the front and back license plates revolve and replace themselves—what had been Georgia plates are now Tennessee, and the plate number has changed as well. Porcupines damn it, that shit is *cool*.

"This way if we get spotted while doing surveillance in Bucksnort, they won't be able to trace it to the vehicle that's registered here at The Hotel Dickson," Mary Sue explains, exploring her role as Captain Obvious, Stator of the Already Apparent Exposition.

She's so excited about this new toy, I'm afraid to ask if the headlights have machine guns installed, out of fear that she'll want me to leave her and the car alone for a few minutes. Fortunately, that must be the end of the technological features of our transport, for Mary Sue ends the presentation with two clicks of the clicker, returning the car to its initial ruby red and Tennessee-plated state.

We get in and Mary Sue begins the drive to Bucksnort. Much to my chagrin, as driver she wins out on the choice of driving music. If I'm going to have to spend the next month listening to non-stop Lady Gaga, I swear I am going to need a lot of fluffy animal toys to massacre.

As we drive, we discuss who to start our surveillance with, and agree Don Anderson is the best person to start with. Charlie, being a truck driver, will be difficult to trail during the day. Clark, being unemployed, might be somewhat easier, but as Don is the leader of the clan and the Klan, we agree to start with him.

About half-way to Bucksnort, on an unoccupied stretch of I-40, Mary Sue pushes the two buttons on her key chain—aside from a slight whirring indicating the changing of the license plates, within the car there is no indication of the change of cosmetic appearance—I have to glance out the window to confirm that the car has indeed changed color again.

When we at last arrive in the tiny town of Bucksnort, we decide to grab some lunch before starting our surveillance. We find a tiny diner right in the center of town—it's the kind of diner which looks like if this were a slasher movie, you all in the audience would be screaming at us not to enter because we'll probably end up being the next items on the menu. Fortunately for Mary Sue and me, this isn't a slasher movie and probably the worst 'secret ingredient' we can expect to find served here is squirrel meat.

As we enter the diner, a bell over the door signaling our entrance, the first thing I notice is a rotund, greasy man sitting at the counter, wearing torn jeans, a camo ball cap, and what was probably once a white wife beater, but is now more of a sickly greenish-grey rag with armholes.

Worse than all of that, though, is the mullet. I. *Hate*. Mullets. Whenever I see anyone with a mullet, it fills me with a blinding rage. And before you inundate me with all that psycho-babble hoopla, no it's *not* just because my abusive ass-hat of a father had a mullet. Jeez. Despite what all you whiny Freuders may think, not *everything* in life comes down to mommy/daddy issues.

The fact that the first thought which came to my head after . . . after my mother killed the bastard was not grief but relief and then wondering if I could get away with shaving his bastard head bald has absolutely no bearing on any of this whatsoever.

Anyway, I recognize the louse at the bar

immediately from the case files: Don Anderson's brother-in-law, Clark Grobe. A quick glance at Mary Sue reveals she has recognized him, also. Aside from a brief glare making it clear strangers are not welcome to stay any longer than necessary in this town, Mr. Grobe completely ignores us—which is just as well for us. It's easier to stalk someone who doesn't pay you any mind.

A blonde waitress steps out of the back, sees us, and says, "Sit wherever y'all like, I'll be right with you."

We make our way to the back of the diner—Clark Grobe is so expansive that we almost don't have enough room to squeeze past him in the aisle between the counter and the booths—and sit at a booth where we can furtively keep an eye on Grobe without being noticed.

The waitress re-emerges, and the grease ball at the counter hollers at her, "Becks, get me some more eggs, will ya?"

"Not now, ya lug, I've got cust'mers," the waitress snaps. I notice the nametag on her uniform reads 'Becky.' This must be Don's younger sister, and therefore wife of the pig at the bar. The apparent fact that Grobe is mooching off of his wife being a waitress while he lives off of welfare checks makes me hate the bastard even more, and I find myself looking more and more forward to killing him by the minute.

"Sorry 'bout that," Becky says, walking up to our booth and handing us each a menu. "Can I start ya off with some drinks?"

We each order a coffee and then Becky leaves us to peruse the menu. I do not see anything listing squirrel meat, but that doesn't necessarily mean anything.

When Becky returns, I order a burger (deciding to take the risk of unlisted squirrel ingredients), and Mary Sue—Cali Girl to the end—orders a salad.

While we wait for our food to finish, we surreptitiously keep an eye on Grobe at the counter, but other than staring at his food grumpily, taking the odd bite, and the occasional release of flatulence, he does nothing of interest, so we are both relieved when Becky brings us our food so that we have something else to focus on.

We eat in silence to avoid drawing any extra attention to ourselves, and also so we can get out of the awkward tension of the diner as quickly as possible. When we're done, we pay up our tab and I make sure to leave Becky a good thirty percent tip. I'm normally a pretty shitty tipper, to be honest, but after seeing what the poor woman has to put up with, I can't help but feel like she deserves something extra.

Before we leave, I notice Mary Sue reach into her purse, pull something out, and then reach far underneath the table—I'd be willing to bet my favorite knife, she just placed a bug under the table so we can listen to the goings on of the diner surreptitiously.

Once back in the privacy of our car, Mary Sue asks, "So . . . do we stick to our plan and go find brother Don, or do we stick around here and keep an eye on the charming Mr. Grobe?"

"We change course," I reply, having already come to the decision while we were in the diner. "I don't believe in Fate or any of that superstitious nonsense, but that doesn't mean I'm going to turn my back on an opportunity the universe drops in my lap. We'll have plenty of time to watch the head of the family later."

"Agreed."

Mary Sue pulls out of the parking lot, and drives down the road just enough so we can still see the diner and anyone coming in or out of it, but not necessarily be conspicuous and noticed from within the diner.

Once parked, Mary Sue pulls out of her bag a pair of wireless earphones and hands one to me, confirming my suspicion that what she placed under the table back at the diner was, indeed, a bug. When we get back to our hotel tonight, we will be able to plug in the serial number of the device Mary Sue planted at the diner into our laptop software, and then everything that happens at the diner will be automatically recorded and saved for us to review later, so we will never miss any crucial information.

I swear, the next several hours go slower than a snail drugged on Valium. Fortunately, we're at the beginning of spring so the weather is not too extreme, otherwise sitting in the car for hours on end would be unbearable. We must have arrived after the lunch rush hour (assuming there even *is* a lunch rush hour in this town . . .) because we don't even really see anyone enter the diner, except for one or two stray customers. Listening to our planted bug doesn't add much relief to the monotony, other than the occasional bark of Grobe making his working wife prepare him more food.

It does, however, make one thing clear to us: chances are, Grobe will be pretty easy to keep tabs on and figure out his daily routine. It looks like pretty much any day that Becky is working, he will be spending his day at the diner—probably simultaneously mooching off of her employer and 'keeping tabs on his woman.'

Shortly before five in the afternoon, a beat-up old truck pulls up to the diner parking lot and a young man looking to be about eighteen jumps out of the truck and enters the restaurant –from our vantage point he appears to be average height, scrawny, with dark hair fashioned in—you guessed it—a mullet. We're too far down the road to be sure, but based off of my recollections of the case files, I'm guessing this is the Grobes's eldest son, Clark Jr.

Over our earpieces, we hear the young man say, "Hey Pa, you ready?"

"What're you boys up to tonight?" Becky asks.

"Not that it's any your bus'ness, woman," Clark Sr. spits, "but we got plans with yer brother."

"Well, fine, but don't stay out too late," Becky replies, apparently used to being treated like a piece of garbage.

"Iffin I wanna stay out late, I'll stay out late, ya hear me?" Clark Sr. snaps.

"Pa, Uncle Donny's waitin' on us," Clark Jr. intervenes.

"Fine," Clark Sr. grumbles, and even over our tiny headphones we can hear the groans of relief from Grobe's chair as he relieves it of his substantial burden.

Without another word, the two Clarks exit the diner. I turn to Mary Sue and say, "Jackpot."

12

WE FOLLOW THE beat-up Grobes truck at a distance so as not to garner too much attention. Fortunately, it's starting to get dark out, which will make it harder for them to distinguish us.

After about a ten-minute drive, we find ourselves approaching the center of town and the truck turns right off of the main road into a parking lot, facilitating a large, white building. Mary Sue parks the car about a block away, and we watch as the two Clarks—easily distinguishable even in the fading twilight by the girth of one and lack of girth of the other—get out of the truck and disappear into the white building.

We wait in the car for about fifteen minutes, to make sure no one else arrives, before getting out and making our way down the block to investigate closer. The parking lot looks to be about half full, so the two Clarks must have been the last of the group to arrive.

As we draw closer to the white building, we begin to see a sign clearly marked at the front of the building: Bucksnort Town Hall.

"You mean to tell me they actually hold K.K.K. meetings in the effing *town hall???*" Mary Sue whispers, indignantly.

"Gotta love the south . . . " is my only response.

We make a loop of the building, sticking to the shadows so as to be less likely to be noticed. Unfortunately, we do not achieve much reconnaissance, due to the fact that the blinds are all drawn. It isn't hard to tell where our query is meeting though, for it's the only room with a light on. We position ourselves outside the window, but although we can make out the sounds of voices coming from within, it's barely a discernible murmur of chatter that we can't really make anything out.

"We're going to need to get this place bugged, if we want to find anything useful out about what they're up to," I whisper to Mary Sue.

"I'll contact Zeke when we get back to the hotel," Mary Sue whispers back. "He can arrange it with the governor to have the whole town hall bugged."

We remain, perched in the shadows under the window, for about an hour, but we would be better off learning to speak cricket if we want to gain any sort of information. I am seriously at the point of losing my mind with boredom, when we suddenly hear the scraping of chairs, followed shortly thereafter by the lights inside the town hall turning out. We quickly, and silently, make our way closer to the front of the building, staying in the shadows and on the side of the building away from the parking lot, so we can observe the men's exit without being observed ourselves.

A dozen men exit the town hall, seven of whom I recognize from the case files as being of the Anderson Klan (Don, Charlie, Clark Sr., Clark Jr., John, Duke and Bobby). The other five men must be friends of the family, or just other members of the Klan. Don Anderson leads the parade out of the town hall.

"So we all agree 'at we'll meet 'gain on the twenty-first, 'fore the event on the twenty-ninth?" Don says, as the last of the men exit and he proceeds to lock up the town hall. The other eleven men mumble agreement. "Good, 'at'll be 'at. See y'all then."

The twelve men shake hands, mumbling various farewells, and then retreat to their respective cars in the town hall parking lot.

Mary Sue and I wait until the last of the tail lights have disappeared into the darkness of the night, before returning to our car.

"Shall we call it a night?" I ask, as we make our way down the block to where we parked.

"Definitely," Mary Sue replies eagerly. "I say we get back to our hotel and get some food, ASAP."

"Ten-four on that, sister."

On the drive back to Dickson—Mary Sue returning the car to its Ruby-Red-Georgian façade as soon as we are on the highway—we discuss what (little) we've learned.

"Okay, so the day wasn't a *complete* waste of time," Mary Sue says, though I can hear the disappointment in her voice.

"Yeah, we learned Clark Sr. is a pig of a husband, and the Anderson Klan and their friends have some event planned for the twenty-ninth, and probably won't be meeting again until the week before. The twenty-first is about a week-and-a-half away . . . I am going to go bat-crazy if we have to wait until then to find out what these ass-hats are up to."

"Well, we'll continue to follow the family, of

course," Mary Sue goes on, "and look for other opportunities and places we can bug for information, but . . . "

"What . . . ?" I can tell from the sound of her voice, she's going to suggest something I won't want to hear.

"Well, it's just probably the easiest way to find out information will be to . . . get to know one of them . . . on a personal level."

Told ya so. Like I've told you before, there is no T.H.E.M. rule restricting operatives from engaging in relationships while on the job, even with marks. I personally try to refrain from partaking in that liberty, due to my aforementioned proclivity to want to kill men I sleep with. However, I must admit that, at least in theory, it could potentially be a useful tool for gathering information which otherwise would be difficult to come by.

Mary Sue, on the other hand, has previously demonstrated she has zero qualms about 'getting her nethers twixed' (her words, not mine) while on assignment. No doubt the fact that she doesn't want to murder every man she sleeps with helps with that endeavor.

"Idunno, Lindsay," I say, hoping I'll be able to talk her out of this course of action. "This could be *really* risky. We're trying to stay under the radar on this one, after all. If we do this, we'll have no choice but to come up with a cover story for our Dupes as well as our Herring."

"Okay, but we will probably need to do that, anyway. Let's be honest. Bucksnort ain't exactly the happenin' social center of the Bible Belt, Nanetta. Our chances of spying on this family for several weeks without getting spotted and asked about what we're doing in town are about nilch."

"Okay, that's true," I begrudgingly admit, "but it doesn't mean we have to go around getting all cozy with the locals."

"On the contrary—if one of us were to start dating one of the younger Anderson men, *that* could be our reason for coming into town so often. We could just continue our cover story that we're staying in Dickson for a few months for a court case, and wanting to get out of the city from time-to-time. Strike up a relationship with one of the younger Anderson men, and see if we can get more information. I've found nothing loosens a guy's tongue faster than the wonders of The Magic Hoo-Ha."

I hate it when she makes a valid point.

"Fine," I resignedly sigh, pinching the bridge of my nose to fight off the headache I feel coming on. "But since you're the one so keen on this idea, you're the one who will be rollin' in the hay with the Apple Dumpling Gang."

"Fine by me," Mary Sue responds with a shrug, as if we were simply debating who got to choose where we were going to eat tonight. "But Nanetta, seriously, how long has it been since you . . . *ahem* . . . had a *Casual Encounter of the Sixty-Ninth Kind?*"

"Oh for the love of fucking Neil Patrick Harris until he turns straight," I groan—I really hate it when she forces me into 'girl talk' like this. "Not that this is any of your business, but I haven't had any 'casual encounters,' sixty-nine or otherwise, since Duluth."

"So . . ."

"Yes, *he* was my last," I refuse to give Nick the

satisfaction of uttering his name, even though he is nowhere nearby.

"Oh honey . . . you gotta correct that, A.S.A.P.," Mary Sue gasps in horror.

"Thanks, but I'm good."

"You're telling me that you're good knowing the last guy who reaped your oats is the same guy hell-bent on killing you? Sorry, but I don't believe that for a second."

"For fuck's sake . . . Lindsay, it's complicated . . . "

"Well, uncomplicate it for me."

Porcupines damn it. Ugh. We've still got at least a twenty minute car ride ahead of us, and Mary Sue clearly is not going to let up on this.

"Look," I groan in defeat, "I've never told you this before, but I have this . . . tendency. Whenever I sleep with a guy, I have a strong desire to kill him afterwards."

"Every time?"

"Just about. It's not so bad after the first time, but if I sleep with a guy more than once . . . the urge is almost unbearable. It's why I don't exactly seek out long-term relationships."

"But what about–"

"Jason was the exception," I respond, curtly enough so that hopefully she will take the hint and leave it alone. For once, she does.

"Ok, fine," she says, moving on from the topic of Jason. "But since we're going to end up killing this mark anyway, why not use him to cleanse your palate and get Nick out of your system? Kill two cocks with one hen, ya know?"

Moving on from Jason and back to Nick—I can't

say this is progress. Even so, I *really* hate it that, once again, she has a fucking point.

"No, it's too risky," I assert, standing my ground. "We can't risk my killing him before we're ready—we're going to do the whole family at once as spree kill, remember?"

"Suit yourself," Mary Sue finally relents with another non-committal shrug. "More fun for me."

I raise no complaint when Mary Sue turns up the Lady Gaga on the radio. I'd much rather endure the Gaga than have to continue more annoying girl talk for the rest of our drive back to Dickson.

13

WHEN WE ARRIVE back at The Hotel Dickson, we are eagerly greeted in the lobby by our friend from the night before, Tim the Bellman.

"Welcome back Ms. Buchanan, Ms. Dieterle, is there anything I can assist you with this evening?" Tim asks, reminding me of a love-sick puppy dog. I can't help if he's hoping to get another of Mary Sue's 'tips.'

"Easy there, Tim," says an older, balding man wearing the same monkey organ-grinder uniform as Tim, stepping between Tim and ourselves. I assume from his reprimand that he's a supervisor or something. "I gather you are our new long-term residents?" The balding man inquires of Mary Sue and myself.

"Yes," Mary Sue says in her thick, fake, southern drawl. "I'm Lindsay Buchanan, and this is my associate Nanetta Dieterle."

"It's a pleasure to meet you," the man replies—as his eyes wander over us, I can feel him undressing us and I have to refrain from visibly shuddering with revulsion. "I am Howard, the head of Guest Services here at The Hotel Dickson. If either of you need anything during your stay with us, please do not hesitate to ask."

"Thank you, Howard," I say, hating the southern accent coming out of my mouth.

Tim, apparently crestfallen at being stepped over by his boss, slouches and returns to behind the bell desk. Howard rolls his eyes in slight irritation, and says, "You'll have to forgive him—he's still in training and has yet to learn the nuances of subtle customer service."

"How long has he been here?" Mary Sue asks.

"Only about a week. Truth is, most of our staff is new. Several months ago the hotel was bought out by a new management company, and they shut it down for a few months to renovate—we actually had our grand re-opening just before you arrived, this past weekend. While they kept a few key personnel on hand—myself included—the new management let go most of the old staff before closing and hired all new staff for the reopening. But enough business, do not let me keep you ladies any longer. Again, should either of you need anything while you are here, please do not hesitate to reach out to me personally."

He hands each of us a business card, and the slithery smile on his face affirms my conviction that if I will be asking anyone for assistance during our stay, it will *not* be the head of Guest Services.

We cross the lobby toward the hotel restaurant, and Mary Sue whispers in my ear, "Sheesh, that Howard's quite a skeeze, huh?"

"Yeah, I got that impression, too," I respond, still unable to shake the feeling he was undressing us with his eyes throughout our conversation.

"But that Tim . . . he's kinda cute, for a twenty year-old. Think he's a virgin?"

"Woman, you need serious help. Honestly, have you looked into Sexaholics Anonymous? Because you really have a problem . . . "

"Oh, come off your high horse," Mary Sue responds, rolling her eyes. "I'm just making up for your prudish chastity."

I can say with absolute certainty this is the first time in my entire life *anyone* has ever referred to me as prudish. I can't say how this makes me feel . . .

"Besides, it's kinda fun deflowering an 'innocent young thing' like that," she continues. "All nervous and cute, but wanting to learn what to do and how to do it. Not like cocky older guys who think they know everything about the castle but can't even find the fucking doorbell."

"Can we please drop this and talk about *work*, for fuck's sake?"

Damn it. I do sound like a prude. *Fuck.*

"Okay, okay. I'm just joking around anyway, trying to get a rise out of you."

While I'm sure that's at least partly true, I'm not entirely convinced she wasn't at least somewhat serious about deflowering the bellboy.

We make quick work of our dinner at the restaurant, wanting to get back to work. I order a burger and fries, Mary Sue another salad. Dinner done, and our bill paid, we return to my room to discuss our plan of action.

First things first, Mary Sue sends Zeke a text message notifying him we need to bug the Bucksnort Town Hall. While she texts, I open up the safe by my bed and retrieve my case files.

"So, first thing we need to decide," I say, laying out

the various files across my bed, "is which of the Anderson Klan boys we're going to target to be our . . . 'informant.'"

Mary Sue separates the four case file photos of the younger men in the family—the brothers John and Duke Anderson, and their cousins, Bobby Anderson, and Clark Grobes Jr.

"Of the four of them," Mary Sue replies, inspecting each photo intently, "I'd say Clark Jr. would be my top pick."

"Of course you'd pick the youngest," I respond, rolling my eyes in disgust. "Honestly, woman, you are one roofied lollipop and a creepy white van short of being a pedophile . . . "

"Ok yes, I like 'em young, but that's not the only reason," Mary Sue huffs defensively. "It's also a tactical decision. Let's be honest, the younger he is, the more impressionable he'll be, and therefore the more likely to let something important slip."

Self-serving though her excuse may be, I concede she has a point.

"Alright, fine. Whatever you want. In that case, let's start looking into young Mr. Grobes's personal life and figure out a way to get you in."

We start looking up everything we can find online about Clark Jr.—primarily utilizing his social media accounts, of course. It always boggles my mind how much information people make publicly available on their social media accounts. Obviously this is a concept that's not exactly my cup of tea. Can you picture me having a Twitter account? 'Well, I de-spleened someone today. Here's a pic of his entrails. Loser didn't even scream. #Lame.' Yeah. That kinda thing may be fun for the president, but even *I* have some social standards.

From all accounts, it appears Clark Jr. is single, which will make things easier for Mary Sue to 'snag' him—though Mary Sue is clearly disappointed by the 'lack of challenge.' When we get back to L.A., I am *definitely* going to look into a sex addicts help group for her, because she clearly has some serious issues (other than, of course, being a deranged, psychopathic serial killer).

Clark Jr. dropped out of high school in his senior year and is currently living in his parents' basement. Based off his various profile status updates, it seems he doesn't do much except play games on his Xbox.

Before we've even realized it, it's nearly midnight. Time flies when you're stalking a lowlife dipshit so you can seduce, find out what he and his fucktard uncles are up to, and then kill him.

We agree to get some rest and reconvene in the morning to figure out the rest of our game plan to snare Clark Jr.

Once Mary Sue has returned to her room, I am suddenly overcome by extreme exhaustion. Weird. I'm a night owl, by nature, and even though it's nearly midnight, I usually don't get this tired so quickly. If I didn't know any better, I'd think someone might have drugged me—but it's been a few hours since we had our dinner, so the only person who could have roofied me was Mary Sue, and I'm pretty sure she didn't drug me.

I change into my P.J.'s, climb into bed, and fall almost instantly asleep.

Unfortunately, it proves to not be a restful sleep

because, once again, my slumber is haunted by the infuriating, looping dream of Jason turning into Nick. For fuck's sake, this is really getting annoying . . .

14

WAKE UP even more tense and sore than I did yesterday. Before anything else, I call the spa and ask when is the soonest they can get me in. The girl on the phone checks her ledger, and then responds that she can squeeze me in, in about 15 minutes. I tell her I'll be right down, then hop in the shower, and practically sprint to the spa.

By pure chance, I'm able to get the same masseuse from the day before, Bill. Hey, just because I won't allow myself to sleep with him, doesn't mean I have to refrain from letting him rub me down in other ways . . .

By the end of my massage, I've made up my mind on a matter I've been toggling in my mind ever since waking up—and I'd be lying if I said hunky Bill didn't have something to do with settling the matter. Mary Sue is going to be unbearable when I confess this decision to her, but it's clear after two nights in a row of dreaming about Jason and Nick that I need to do something to make these dreams stop before I go insane. Well . . . *more* insane . . .

After my massage, I return to my room, finding Mary Sue waiting for me in the hall.

Once we are inside the relative safety of my room, I tell her, "Alright, I'm in."

"What do you mean?" she asks, confusion etched in every line of her face.

"I'm going to join you on your . . . *dating* exploit with the Anderson boys in Bucksnort. I need to get Nick out of my system, and if I'm going to risk succumbing to the urge to kill a random palate cleanser, it might as well be someone who's already on the chopping block, anyway."

I watch in utter horror as her face slowly morphs from confusion, to comprehension, to deathly, exuberant, excitement. She begins jumping up and down with such veracity, I fear for her safety (and mine).

"Oh, *Nanetta!* This is great! OMG, I'm so excited! We are going to have so much *fun!* The Psycho Sisters hitting up the town and slaying the dudes—*literally!* Oh, I can't *wait!*"

"Please don't make me regret this decision, already," I implore her. She ignores me.

"Oh, we're gonna have to go shopping, pick up new outfits, get new shoes, we're going to absolutely *kill* those hicks . . . "

She continues on her inane babbling of word vomit, but I tune her out. There's only so much Mary Sue I can take at a time without wanting to strangle her.

"Okay, okay, but first we need to finish up our game plan," I interrupt, unable to take any more of her blabber.

"Yeah, yeah, you're right," she sighs resignedly.

While Mary Sue retrieves her laptop from her

room, I lay out the case files across my bed. Mary Sue sets up shop with her laptop at the foot of my bed and continues trying to find out as much about Clark Jr. as possible, while I begin thinking about my target. Choosing who I want to target is easy—Duke Anderson is the oldest of the younger generation of men, only a few years younger than me, and—most important of all—he's the only one who doesn't sport a mullet, so there's a slightly higher chance I'll be able to resist killing him before we're ready.

Before long, we are ready to compare our notes.

Like Clark Jr., Duke is availably single, so no issues on that front. Aside from their white supremacist extra-curricular activities, the age difference between the two cousins is apparently large enough that they don't really interact much, socially. Where Clark Jr. is a basement-dwelling high school dropout, Duke actually graduated and is living in an apartment, while working full time at his dad's car repair shop. Based on his profile photos and status updates, it seems Duke spends most of his free time either at his favorite watering hole bar, or fishing.

Even Mary Sue admits at this point that I ended up picking the better of the two cousins. Duke is still nowhere near the kinda guy I would approach, even for just a palette cleanser, if I had a choice in the matter. But if I can't saddle up with hunky Bill the masseuse, and have to choose from any of the Anderson men, Duke's definitely the pick of the litter.

"So, next question," Mary Sue proceeds after we are done comparing notes, "do we go about nabbing these two boys subtly and take our time getting to know them, or–"

"Or the direct approach?" I finish for her.

"Exactly."

"I vote for the direct approach. Hit them up, tell them we're here in the area for a short while on business and wanting to have some fun on the side when we're not working, and ask if they're interested. They're men under thirty—I doubt either of them would refuse an offer like that."

"I like it. Skip beating around the bush and get right down to beating inside the bush."

I roll my eyes, but just say, "Yeah, something like that. And let's try to keep each of them from finding out about us dating them—they don't seem that close anyway, so they probably won't be doing any locker talk together, but just tell them due to the high profile nature of our case we need them to be quiet about our relationship."

"I'm in, let's do it," we return to our laptops and begin laying our traps.

T.H.E.M. of course provides operatives with a full complement of fake social media profiles for their Dupes while on assignment. I log into the Facespace account for Nanetta Dieterle, and send a friendship request to Duke Anderson, along with the following message:

"Hey, I'm staying in Dickson for a while on business and was hoping to find someone local to hang out with in my downtime—nothing serious, just casual company while I'm in the area. I see you're not too far away, so thought you might want to hang out. Like I said, I'm here for work, but I should be free most evenings and weekends. I know, this probably sounds like a fishing scam or something, but I promise I'm for real. Anyway, if you're interested, let me know. I'd love to meet up and see where things go."

For an extra touch, I add a kissy-face emoji. My work is nothing if not subtle.

I read over it one more time—probably more correct grammar and spelling than Duke is used to seeing, but it fits in with my character of a law assistant, so I leave it as is and hit the send button. It also carefully toes the line between being flirtatious and insinuating what I'm looking for, without being a brazen harlot—again, keeping everything within the character of a professional legal assistant who also has physical needs she wants met.

A few seconds later, a satisfied *click* coming from Mary Sue's laptop indicates she, as well, is done sewing her seeds of seduction. Knowing Mary Sue's libido, I assume her message was somewhat more brazen than mine—which, I must admit, will probably work just fine on the barely-adult, basement-dwelling Clark Jr.

"And now . . . we wait," Mary Sue says, as she closes her laptop with a satisfied snap.

"Now, we wait," I confirm, dreading this endeavor, but resolute in my decision to do whatever I need to in order to stop having these fucking dreams about Nick and Jason.

15

I CAN'T CLAIM to be surprised Mary Sue gets a response from Clark Jr. before noon. Considering that Clark Jr. is a basement-dwelling loser, he probably has spent every day since dropping out of high school having wet dreams imagining getting such an e-mail. There's a reason I didn't even try to place a bet on who would get first response.

"wow, ur super hawt! im total down for w/e you wanna do so hit me up babe," I read the response from Clark Jr. over Mary Sue's shoulder.

"I guess you're gonna be heading over to his basement to jump him right now, then?" I smirk.

"Geez, Nanetta, I'm not a *total* whore, you know. I'm still gonna make him work for it. That's half the fun," Mary Sue replies—despite the sarcasm, I sense I may have actually hurt her feelings. Worst of all, I feel guilty about it. Porcupines damnit. I hate feeling guilty.

"I'm sorry, I didn't mean anything. I was just teasing."

"It's okay, hon, we're good," Mary Sue replies, brushing off my apology with a smile to show me all really is forgiven.

I watch over her shoulder as Mary Sue types up a response to Clark Jr.

"Hang on there, champ. Let's not totally rush into things here. I need to know you're not a serial killer or anything after all! LOL! Can we meet for coffee or something, before deciding if we want to take things further?"

I have a clear mental image of Clark Jr. sitting in his parents' basement, eagerly eyeing his computer or phone waiting for the next message from the beautiful and mysterious Lindsay Buchanan, wearing nothing but his underwear (okay, probably not even wearing *that*, but this is my mental image I'm projecting, and I'd rather not vomit, thank you very much).

Sure enough, hardly any time has passed before she gets another response.

"sure baby. w/e you want. theres a cofe place not far. when you off?"

I sure as hell ain't a Grammar Nazi, but porcupines, this guy makes me understand those people's point of view.

"I should be finished around 5, so say we meet around 6:30?" Mary Sue types back.

"sounds good to me, baby," his response comes back almost immediately.

"Great! I'll be wearing a light blue sweater and jeans," Mary Sue types back.

"what you wearing under?"

"*Barf,*" I respond, gagging after reading Clark Jr.'s latest message.

Mary Sue rolls her eyes, apparently that comment was too far even for her, but she types Lindsay's response anyway, "That's for me to know and you to find out, big guy. ;)"

"For the love of Captain Hammer's Nipples, I sure as *fuck* hope Duke has more class than this schmuck," I groan, still gagging on bile in the back of my throat.

"That won't take much," Mary Sue concedes, before typing one last message to her Don Juan Pathetique: "Hey hon, I gotta get back to work now, but send me the address of the coffee shop and I'll see you there. I look forward to meeting you!"

"sure thing," he responds, again practically immediately, followed by the address of the coffee shop. "c u tonigt. ;) ;)"

Worse than even the deplorable grammar and spelling, the double winky face sends a chill of disgust down my spine, for the lewd insinuation of those smug emoticon bastards is quite apparent.

"Porcupines, are you *really* going to fuck that scumbag?" I ask in disgust.

"I admit, I'm looking less and less forward to the prospect," Mary Sue admits, and I'm relieved to know I'm not the only one bothered by the creep. "But we need information, and let's be honest. If *any* of the Anderson men are going to let something slip about what they're up to, it's going to be this fucktard. And nothing loosens up a man's tongue faster than Magic Lady Bits."

"I *definitely* do not want to see *that* card trick . . . " I respond, laughing despite myself.

Now that Mary Sue's bait has been bitten, we wait for my hook to catch something.

I'll be honest with you. *Please* don't tell Mary Sue this, but I start to feel a tad self-conscious that she got a response faster than I did. I tell myself it's just because Clark Jr. is a loser living in his parents' basement who has nothing better to do with his time than alternating between Xbox games and pleasuring himself, and Duke is just taking longer to respond because he actually has a job and a life, but no matter how much I try, I can't believe it, not one-hundred percent.

There is that nagging, insecure and self-conscious part of me that feels like the reason I haven't gotten a response is because, somehow, Duke can sense I am damaged goods. That I have been tainted for having fallen for Nick Jin's seductions in Duluth, and even a single man in his twenties wouldn't be interested in an offer of an easy, no-strings-attached relationship with me.

That frustrating part of me, more than anything else, firms my resolve to follow through with this. More than anything else, I need to prove to myself that Nick hasn't ruined me. I *will* get past this and I *will* stop having dreams about Nick, even if it means I have to fuck every hillbilly redneck in Tennessee until I can't walk straight and keep myself from killing each and every last one.

While we wait, Mary Sue passes the time reading through Clark Jr.'s Facespace profile history— gathering a more detailed mental picture than the general summary she has compiled so far. I, however, am too anxious to settle for anything so mundane. I sit at the edge of the bed, trying not to fidget, aimlessly flipping through channels on the TV, unable to settle on anything as I don't even know what it is I *want* to watch.

Finally, a little after two in the afternoon, my laptop *dings*, signaling an incoming Facespace message.

"idunno," Duke writes, "this sounds a bit sketchy tbh. can we meet for coffee or something first? someplace public"

Already off to a better start than Mary Sue and Clark Jr.

I don't imagine there are many coffee shops in Bucksnort, and since Mary Sue is the one licensed to drive, I make the quick decision that I should make him come to me here in Dickson so as to avoid the probability of Duke and Clark Jr. seeing each other if we were to meet at the same coffee shop. Also, of the two cousins, Duke is the more likely to have a car and be able to come to me.

"Of course, I wouldn't have it any other way," I type back. "I'm staying at the Hotel Dickson—there's a Buckstars on the corner. Want to meet there, say around 7 tonight?"

Several minutes pass, much more time than it took for Clarky Boy to make up *his* mind, before Duke responds, "alright. but just so ya know, i'll be carryin', just in case you turn out to be a dude or somethin'."

Fucking rednecks and their guns. I never fancied killing with guns. Being a P.S.K. I would often have to concede and kill with a gun if the killer I was profiling would do so, but to me there is no kill greater than the knife. Plunging a blade into the soft, moist flesh of a man—or woman, if need be—I tell ya, there's nothing more satisfying in all the world.

But Nanetta Dieterle is not Sarah Killian. Based on the profile I have created for Nanetta so far, I have to admit she would probably be a good, Southern Christian, gun-toter. I don't like Nanetta.

"LOL!" I type back. "No worries, darlin', I'll be carrying, too, just in case you turn out to be Jack the Ripper or something."

Again, several minutes pass before Duke responds. I get the feeling he is more careful about choosing his words than his primordial cousin, and that's why he takes longer to respond.

"lol! sounds fair to me," he responds at last. "look forward to meeting you."

"You, too! See you at 7!" I respond.

"Well, that takes care of our dates for the night!" Mary Sue responds, chipperly jumping off the bed after having read my conversation with Duke. "Guess I should go start getting ready for mine. I guess you've probably already made a trip to the spa today, yes?"

I sheepishly nod affirmatively.

"Well, then I won't ask you to join me," Mary Sue responds. "We don't need Zeke to murder you the second he gets the bill for this trip . . . Toodles!"

And at that, Mary Sue skips—*literally* skips—out of my room to go get ready for her date with the Neanderthal.

Despite every natural tendency in my body, I find myself looking forward to this date. I haven't been on an actual *date* since . . . porcupines . . . *Jason*. I have never been the dating type anyway. I had one boyfriend in high school—he ended up spread out over most of Los Angeles County, in various pieces (he was technically my *second* murder).

After that, I kinda stayed away from the dating scene, until Jason. Whenever I needed sex, I would just go out and find it. Look, I'm a reasonably attractive woman in her late twenties who lives in Los Angeles. If I want a night of meaningless sex, I can find it. And considering my tendency to want to murder anyone I sleep with, meaningless sex is about all I can afford. Going out and getting to know someone doesn't do me much good, if I'm just going to end up wanting to kill them.

Jason, as you know, was the one exception to that rule, and he had to fuck everything up by going out and being a cheating bastard douchebag. Fucking *ass*assins.

But in any event, after what happened with Nick, I guess I feel like something a bit more wholesome—more *real*—is needed, for the moment at least. I'm still going to end up wanting to kill Duke Anderson, I'm sure, and I know I will enjoy it as much as I have enjoyed killing anyone else, but for now, I think he might be just the palate cleanser I need to get over this fucking mess of emotions and feelings of inadequacy Nick Jin has created.

After this brief tryst with 'real' dating, I tell myself, I will return to my normal, sociopathic self, only seeking out the occasional and most basest form of human connections. Everything will be back to normal, and then I will find Nick Jin and cut his balls off before I slit his throat from ear to ear.

16

MARY SUE PAYS me a brief visit before she heads out for her date shortly before 6:00. As she had promised, she is sporting a blue sweater and casual, but nice, jeans. She looks perfect for the role of young woman headed out for coffee with a blind date.

"Good luck with your date tonight, girlfriend," she chirps. "I'd tell ya to be careful, but I know you, so I won't bother."

"Yeah, you too," I say, rolling my eyes, but smiling.

"Don't jump the kid's bones right away. Make him work for it."

"Ummm . . . shouldn't it be *you* getting that advice?"

"Normally, yes. But with this dipshit, I don't think it will require much restraint on my part to make him wait . . . "

"True that."

"Meet back here when we're done and compare notes?"

"Yeah, I guess."

If we were just comparing work notes about the case, I wouldn't have any hesitation about meeting up afterward. However, I know Mary Sue well enough to know this comparison of notes is going to be more focused on 'girl talk' and less on anything to do with our case. Blargh.

"See you then, girlfriend!" Mary Sue chirps, and then scampers off toward the elevator and her date with the Mr. K.K.K. Man.

I had just gotten out of the shower when Mary Sue stopped by, so I am currently only wearing a hotel bathrobe. I close the door and lay out on my bed the various outfits Nanetta has been supplied with by the T.H.E.M. wardrobe department.

I have to admit, I'm out of my element here. Like I've said already, I have never been much for dating. With the exception of Jason and my one high school boyfriend, dating for me has consisted of a two, maybe three, times a year going out to a bar and finding some random dipshit to take me back to his place and have moderate-to-sometimes decent drunken sex with.

Picking an outfit for that kind of dating is easy. It's not like it takes a lot to convince a guy to have random sex with you. As they say, less is more.

But how to dress when you want to pretend like you actually want to get to know someone . . . for fuck's sake, I don't like getting to know *anyone*. Hell, I've been dragged kicking and screaming into getting to know Mary Sue, I certainly don't know how to go about wanting to get to know a *guy*.

I decide to just copy Mary Sue's lead, and settle on a sweater (light purple instead of blue) and jeans. My natural instinct would be to overdo the make-up, but since I'm trying to break free of my natural instinct for a bit, I decide to go for a more subtle approach. I look at myself in the large closet door mirror, and see a typical 'girl next door' staring back at me. A complete stranger, in every possible way.

Normally, I would be repulsed by this change in myself, and would only put up with it for the sake of the job, baring my teeth all the while. But something has changed in me . . . I want to say I hope it's just a temporary change until I've successfully put Nick behind me, but there is a small part—a *very* small part—that hopes it isn't temporary. I *hate* that part of me, almost more than I hate Nick. Almost.

My makeover complete, I open up my safe of case files and retrieve a revolver provided by T.H.E.M. and place it in my purse—fulfilling my promise to Duke that Nanetta would also be carrying protection of the lethal-non-sexual variety. I then pull on my coat and head out of the hotel. The winter air is brisk, but I remind myself that down here in Tennessee it's a *lot* warmer than it would be if I were still in Minnesota (had that assignment not ended prematurely thanks to Nick Jin's interference, I *would* still be in Minnesota), so I'm grateful for that, at least.

I arrive at the Buckstars on the corner about fifteen minutes early for my date, so I order a latte and find a seat in the back corner of the café, enjoying a few moments of introverted solitude before I have to put on my extrovert act. Back when I was a kid, my mother signed me up in some drama classes at the local community theater. At the time, I hated it and wanted nothing more than to be anywhere else than there. But now I must admit, if nothing else, those classes helped me learn how to pretend to be an extrovert instead of an introvert, on occasion.

At almost precisely 7:00, a tall, bearded man enters the café, and I recognize him immediately from the various case file and online profile photos I've been studying of Duke Anderson. His dark curly hair is slicked back, still drying from a recent shower, it seems. His beard covers most of his face, but is well-groomed. He's at least six feet tall and his build is bulky, but even from across the café I can tell that bulk is more muscle than flab.

Even though he is definitely not my usual type, I would be lying if I didn't admit he was moderately attractive, at least.

He does a quick scan of the coffee shop, and when our eyes meet, I call upon my inner-extrovert, put on my biggest smile, and wave him over to me.

"Nanetta?" he says after crossing to my table, his Tennessee drawl thick and heavy.

"Yes, Duke," I say, putting on my own affected accent. "It's a pleasure to meet you, I'm glad you agreed to meet me."

"Yeah, well I can see you ain't a dude, for sure ma'am," he says, pulling off his coat, draping it on the chair across from me, and sitting down, "but I still can't say I ain't a bit suspicious. You promise the *Dateline* online predators camera crew ain't hidin' in here somewhere, waitin' to jump out at me and yell 'surprise!'?"

I laugh flirtatiously, an utterly foreign feeling in my throat, and say, "No, no. I know it seems sketchy and all, a pretty girl messaging you outta the blue an' all, wantin' to have fun while she's in town."

"Yeah, it does," he admits. "Kinda thing you hear about guys getting scammed for all the time."

"Yeah, I know," laughing that alien flirtatious laugh again. "It's just I travel a lot for my work, so I don't get to stay any one place for long, and it's hard to develop any kind of serious relationship when you're always moving around like that. But I'm still a girl in the prime of my life, so I try to still have a social life—however fleeting—wherever I am. I'm not saying I'm gonna take you back to my hotel room or anything like that, sugar, just it's nice to make some friends while I'm in town. If anything else comes of it . . . well, we can cross that bridge when it comes to it."

"I get that. What do you do that has you travellin' all over like that? Flight attendant or somethin'?"

"No, no. I work for a high profile law firm. They have cases all over the country, so I often get sent wherever their current biggest case is. Usually only a month or two, sometimes longer if the particular case warrants it. Basically, I'm always in town long enough to go completely bat crazy if I don't have some sort of social life, but at the same time not long enough to actually develop anything serious. And so here we are."

"Here we are," he repeats. "I'm guessin' you prob'ly can't talk much about the case you're here on?"

"No, that would be a *big* taboo," I say, laughing again. "Also—because of the case and all, I have to ask you to be discreet about us. The last thing I need is to put egg on the face of my law firm that could potentially influence the trial in any way."

"Sure, that makes sense."

"But I don't really want to talk about work anyway—I spend all day thinkin' and talkin' work, so I'm lookin' for someone to escape that with."

"Understand," is all he says in response. A man of few words—the best kind of man, in my opinion.

"What about you? What do you do?" Who am I, and what have I done with myself?

"My Pa owns a car repair shop, and I work there as one of his mechanics. Pays the bills fer now, and when Pa retires, he's gone give the bus'ness to me, so that'll be somethin' for to look forward to."

He orders a coffee for himself, and another latte for me, and we continue to talk idly, sharing stories about our lives (mine mostly made up, of course). The more we talk, the more distanced I feel from this woman who seems to have possessed my body. That part of me (which I'm just going to go ahead and start calling Nanetta) that I hate seems to have taken control, which I have to admit is just as well. The *real* me—Sarah—would not fare well at this whole 'getting to know you' Julie Andrews bullshit.

Before I even realize how much time has passed, Duke looks at his watch and says, "Lord, it's almost half-past eight. I gotta get goin'—I gotta be at the shop first thing the mornin'."

"Oh my, time does fly, doesn't it? Look, I'm glad you decided to come out here and meet me, Duke."

"I'm glad too, Nanetta."

"Please, call me Nanny."

Nanny? For the love of all that is unholy, I would kill Nanetta if she weren't myself.

"Alright, Nanny."

"I'd like to see you again, Duke, if that's alright with you."

"I'd like that very much, myself, Nanny."

The way he says Nanny, in his thick southern

drawl, makes Sarah want to puke and Nanetta swoon. Instead of resolving the conflicted emotions I've been feeling over the last few days, this is complicating them. Porcupines damnit.

I make a silent note *never* to let Mary Sue know about this nickname. I would never live it down.

"How about tomorrow night?" I ask. His face drops, ever-so-slightly, betraying his hesitation at meeting again so soon. "Sorry if I'm coming on strong here, hon. It's just, I don't know how long I'll be in the area for, so I want to make the most of my time here. And, to be honest, my only other alternative for the night will be to sit in my room watching pay-per-view movies—and I swear I'm gonna go bat-shit if I have to spend another night like that."

For a second, I'm worried I've gone too far, but Duke just laughs and says, "Yeah, I guess I'd be the same if'n I were in yer shoes."

"I'm pretty sure you couldn't fit those big feet into my tiny shoes," I respond with a wink. In my head, Sarah imagines a long, slow, drawn-out death for Nanetta, possibly involving a wiffle bat.

Duke laughs again and says, "I'm gonna have to keep my eye on yeh, I can see. Yer trouble, missy."

"You have *no* idea."

"Alright, yeh talked me into it. Same time, same place?"

"Same bat time same bat channel."

"A *Batman* reference? Nanny, yer a woman after my own heart."

I'm really regretting having invented the 'Nanny' nickname.

"I bet you say that to all the girls. Anyway, I don't

want to hold you any longer, I know you have to get going. So I'll see you here tomorrow night?

"I look forward to it."

We rise and hug—something in Nanetta's gut flutters excitedly at the contact—before donning our respective coats and exiting the café. He offers to walk me back to my hotel, but I tell him not to trouble himself. We hug again—and again, that annoying flutter in Nanetta's gut—and I return to my hotel room, strip out of my clothes and re-adorn the hotel bathrobe.

I sit in silence, trying to tell myself I'm enjoying the solitude, but something feels . . . missing. Fucking a'. I blame Mary Sue for all of this. Until she came into my life, I was happy with my isolated, antisocial, sociopathic life.

Speak of the Devil, shortly after nine, Mary Sue knocks on my door, returning from her date. I can tell almost immediately by her exhausted posture that her date went about as well as I would have expected.

"O.M.G., Nanetta, you would not *believe* . . . I mean God, it was like I was on my first date in middle school, the only difference being that now I'm smart enough to know when a guy is only interested in getting in my pants. Honestly, that naiveté actually made my first middle school date a more tolerable experience than this farce was. All I can say is thank God it's winter, because if it'd been summer and I was wearing a sun dress instead of jeans, that fucking feel-happy creep would've gotten to third base right there in the fucking coffee shop. Which isn't to say I've never gone to third in a coffee shop before, but crikey, not on the first date, *obviously*. Anyway, how was *your* date?"

"It was fine," I say dismissively, hoping to achieve nonchalance. Unfortunately, Mary Sue perks up like a meerkat which has detected something interesting on the prairie.

"*Fine?* That's all? I insist, tell me more, tell me more, like did he drive a car?"

I roll my eyes. "Oh, for the love of Captain Hammer's nipples. Yes, that's all. We met for coffee. We talked. I played the whole 'wanting to get to know you' game. He was . . . nice enough. I guess."

"*Nice enough*? Well fuck me in the ass with a splintery wooden spoon and call me Sally Struthers . . . Sarah Killian, you little goodie-girl, you *like* this guy, don't you?"

"Will you *please* not use my fucking real name while we are on assignment? And *no*, I *do not* like Duke Anderson. He's a low-life hillbilly hick who I wouldn't even give a passing glance to if it weren't for this damn mission."

"Okay, okay. Sorry about the *eal-ray ame-nay* thing. I got carried away. As for *Duke* . . . say what you will, but I think *Nanetta's* got herself a crush—a bit of hillbilly fever, if ya will."

"Shut up before I give *you* hillbilly fever."

It's a weak-ass retort if I ever made one, made even weaker by the fact I can't bring myself to make eye-contact with Mary Sue.

"Fine, fine, miss crabby pants. Whatever you say. I'll just leave you alone, clearly it's past your bedtime. I won't lie, I could use a *long* bleach bath before bed to wash off the feeling of Clark Jr.'s groping fingers . . . Meet for breakfast in the morning? After your obligatory spa appointment, of course."

"Yeah, sure," I respond, not wanting to open up the can of worms that will be the discussion of why I hope I won't *need* to go to the spa in the morning.

"See ya then, girlfriend!" she chirps, and then saunters out of my room to her own.

I set the deadbolt behind her and, fuming, change into my pajamas. Porcupines, Mary Sue pisses me off when she gets under my skin like this. And it pisses me off even more that I *let* her get under my skin.

The fact she is *right*, and her being right means I have also let Duke get under my skin, does nothing to alleviate my foul mood.

As I turn off the lights and climb into bed, far earlier than would be normal for me, I hope my foul mood will prevent any dreams from penetrating my subconscious tonight. It is a futile hope.

17

THE DREAM, of course, continues to haunt my sleeping hours. There is, however, one significant change to the dream. Tonight, Jason's role in the dream has been replaced by Duke. It goes without saying this change does nothing to alleviate the tension caused by my nocturnal imaginings—if anything else, when I at last wake in the morning, I am more tense than I have been so far this week.

I groan, every muscle in my body straining in protest as I role over in bed, pick up the phone and make a spa appointment for half an hour from now. Take a shower, send a text message to Mary Sue letting her know I'll be ready for breakfast in about an hour, and then head down to the spa. I'm a little disappointed to find Bill the Hunky Masseuse is not available today, but I suppose they have to give him a day off from time-to-time. His replacement this morning is a girl named Tiffany, and while she doesn't work out all of the knots the way Bill the Hunky Masseuse would, I grudgingly admit she gets the job done, for all intents and purposes.

After my massage, I meet Mary Sue for breakfast at the hotel restaurant.

"Goodness, Nanetta," she says, as I sit down at the table she has been holding for us. "You keep this up and you're going to disappear into that spa before we're done here."

"Lindsay, I'm not in the mood."

"Well, I see a good night's sleep did nothing to cure your cheery temperament," she snaps.

"Maybe that's because I haven't *had* a good night's sleep since we got here."

Within an instant, Mary Sue's brow snaps from irritated to concerned.

"Why not?" she asks.

Damn it. I should've kept my mouth shut. She'll never let up until I tell her something, now.

"I've been having . . . dreams . . . "

"So what? Dreams shouldn't be enough to ruin an entire night's sleep."

"It's not just that I'm dreaming . . . it's what I'm dreaming about . . . "

"And *that* would be . . . ?"

Fuck, the restaurant is the *last* place I want to get into this, but I set my own trap in this instance.

"I'm dreaming about Nick," I respond, bitterly. If you think I'm going to talk about the *other* aspect of my dream—the Jason/Duke part—you're fucking nuts.

Mary Sues face falls into one of sad compassion— and it makes me want to scream. I don't need pity from anyone, least of all her.

"Oh . . . shit, that sucks," is all she can come up with.

"Yeah, well . . . I think you can understand why I'm not in the best of spirits after dreaming about *that* all night long for three nights in a row."

117

"Yeah, I can."

The rest of our breakfast is spent in relative silence—it says something about the situation that even Mary Sue can't come up with words for it.

As we return to our rooms, Mary Sue breaks the awkward, but welcomed, silence and asks, "So . . . we planning on making dates again for tonight?"

"I . . . already have . . . " I quietly admit.

As a testament to our—admittedly tenuous—friendship, the only response I get from Mary Sue is a sly, sideways eye glance. Sometimes, she does know when to bite her tongue, and I greatly appreciate it when she does.

We get to my room, and once inside she says, "So, obviously we can't just sit around the hotel all day waiting for our dates."

"Fuck no, I'll go insane. Well . . . *more* insane . . . "

"Same here. So shall we make a trip to Bucksnort for some more surveillance?"

"Definitely. But we'll have to be careful. We don't want Clark Jr. or Duke to see us."

"Right. So we'll stay away from Don's car shop, since Duke'll probably be there."

"He will. He mentioned last night he was working today."

"Right. And we'll stay away from the Grobes's house, since I can just about guarantee that's where Clark Jr. will be spending his entire day."

"Indeed. Following Charlie isn't practical, what with him being a truck driver and all. So that leaves us with following Clark Grobe Sr.—who probably will be spending the day stalking his wife at the diner again, assuming she's working—John Anderson, or Bobby Anderson."

"I vote for either John or Bobby. We already have surveillance on the diner established, so if Clark Sr. does anything out-of-the ordinary today, then we can decide if it warrants keeping a closer eye on him."

"Agreed. Alright, let's start looking into John and Bobby then, see if we can find out where they might be today? I presume you want Bobby being the younger one?"

"God no," Mary Sue replies in disgust. "I'm afraid to say Clark Jr. has taken away the joy of cradle robbing—for now, at least. So I'll look up John, thank you very much."

"Okay, but you don't get to trade up your mark if you decide you like John better than Clark Jr. No take-backsies in this game."

Mary Sue rolls her eyes, and retorts, "Yeah, yeah. You probably just want the two brothers for yourself."

"No thanks," I reply curtly. "Refraining from killing *one* of these hillbillies is going to be difficult enough for me—and I've seen John Anderson's mullet. It's the mulletest mullet of all mullets—I definitely would not be able to resist cutting off his head if I slept with him. Besides, a three-way is *nowhere* on my bucket list. One penis at a time is *more* than enough, thank you very much."

"God, Nanetta, you sound like my fucking grandmother. Honestly, you don't know what you're missing, girlfriend."

"Please do not elaborate on that. We're already treading dangerously close to T.M.I. territory."

"Okay, okay. Shall we get to work then?"

"Please."

She goes to her room and returns a few moments

later with her laptop, and we set to work. First things first, Mary Sue sets up another date with Clark Jr. for tonight at their coffee shop. Needless to say, Clark Jr. responds almost instantly with none of the hesitation Duke showed last night at my request for an immediate second date.

That detail out of the way, we move on to research. Since we're not trying snare either of these marks in a web of seduction, we don't have to be quite as exhaustive in our research. Within an hour, we both have compiled a profile of each of our marks and are ready to compare notes.

John—Duke's younger brother—is twenty-three, and works in a second-hand CD store. Bobby is twenty-three and, similar to John, he works in a StopGame video game store (I wouldn't be surprised if Clark Jr. takes advantage of his cousin's store employee discount). Based off of their Facespace profiles, both John and Bobby have girlfriends, which makes it just as well we decided to go after Clark Jr. and Duke instead (though I gather Mary Sue is still second-guessing her decision—even I would probably prefer getting tangled in a sordid affair over having to deal with the molestations of Clark Jr.).

"Honestly, there's not much difference between these two, as far as just picking which one to spy on," Mary Sue sighs, after we've finished sharing our findings.

"When all else fails," I say, reaching into my purse and pulling out a quarter, "heads or tails?"

"Head, always," Mary Sue replies with a coy wink.

I ignore her innuendo, and flip the coin into the air.

"Tails," I reply, once the coin has landed in the

palm of my hand. "We'll tail Bobby today, and John tomorrow, unless something else comes up. Sound like a plan?"

"Sounds like a plan, girlfriend! To the Skank Mobile!"

"We are *not* calling the car *that*," I reply, curtly rising and heading toward the door.

"Whatever you say, grandma," Mary Sue retorts, following behind me.

In case you couldn't tell, I don't have a religious bone in my body. Even so, I pray—to who or what, I don't know—for patience so that I don't slit Mary Sue's throat (and void my contract with T.H.E.M. in the process) before this mission is over.

18

AS WE DRIVE to Bucksnort, Mary Sue turns to me and asks, "You know you're going to have to kill him right?"

"Who? Tom Cruise? Yes, I know. It was written in the stars, that someday our paths will cross and I will have to kill him. I'm okay with this fate. In fact, I welcome it. The smug little prick deserves it."

"No, you silly ninny," she chides, rolling her eyes. "Duke. You're going to have to kill him at the end of this."

I know where she's going with this, but I'm not going to make it easy for her.

"No shit, Sherlock. That's the whole reason we're here, isn't it?"

"Yes, exactly. And if you're starting to like him, won't that make it harder for you to kill him?"

"For the last time, *I don't like him*. He is a backwoods, trailer-park hick, and the only reason I'm seeing him at all is because of the mission. When I slit his throat, it will be no different to me than the hundreds of other people I've killed while on assignment."

"Fine, fine. So you say. But, just hypothetically, say

you *did* end up liking him . . . would that change anything when the end of the mission comes?"

I sigh with resignation. Clearly, she is not going to give up easily on this.

"Hypothetically, if that *were* to happen, which it *won't*, no. I've never had any qualms about killing people I liked in the past."

This isn't entirely true. Back in Duluth, there was one student I'd had to kill because he saw something he shouldn't have and would have compromised the mission if I'd let him live. I'd liked that kid, though obviously not in a *romantic* way, and killing him was not easy for me. But Mary Sue doesn't need to know about all that (she was temporarily unconscious at the time when it happened).

"Most of the men I killed before T.H.E.M. recruited me were men I'd slept with, after all, and so I must have liked them at least a little."

My definition of 'like' is a loose one. As a general rule, I hate everyone who isn't me. However, there are some people I hate less than others, and if I'm going to drop my pants for a guy he has to be slightly lower on the Scale of Hate than most people.

"Okay, hon, whatever you say," Mary Sue says, but doubt riddles her words. "Just want to make sure you don't hurt yourself, or anything."

"Life is nothing but hurt, Lindsay. I learned that the hard way. Besides, I'm a big girl. I can take care of myself."

"Certainly won't argue *that* point," Mary Sue concedes.

The rest of the ride is spent with me listening to Mary Sue singing along with the radio, more or less in key. But I don't complain, because that is definitely preferable to heart-to-heart girl talk.

We arrive in Bucksnort and drive up to the StopGame store where Bobby Anderson works, but before we pull into the parking lot, Mary Sue curses under her breath and speeds past the store.

"Ummm . . . that was our stop, Lindsay," I mutter, confused.

"Did you see that bicycle outside?" she asks, irritation straining her voice.

"Didn't really get a chance to look that closely, to be honest . . . "

"Well, I'm pretty sure that was Clark Jr.'s bike. It at least looks like the one he rode to meet me at the coffee shop last night, in any event."

"Of course. Parents' basement. Mooches off of his cousin's employee discount to get cheap video games. No job. No girlfriend. No car, so he has to get around on bicycle when his parents' truck isn't free. The picture is becoming clearer and clearer. Well, at least he gets *some* exercise then instead of morphing into a full-fledged coach potato."

"Ya know, you don't *have* to keep pointing out I drew the short straw this time."

"Please. As if you wouldn't be doing the same if it was the other way around."

"Fair enough. In any event, I suggest we change plans and tail John today, Bobby tomorrow. It's not worth the risk to wait around for Clark Jr. to leave the store, since he might see us when he leaves."

"Agreed. Let's just hope he doesn't spend every day at the game store."

"I don't think that'll be a problem. No job,

remember? His parents give him a bit of money for helping with the house from time-to-time, and that's the entirety of his spending money."

The change in tactic doesn't cost us much time—as I've stated before, Bucksnort ain't exactly a metropolis, so a few minutes later we are pulling up to the second-hand CD store where John Anderson works.

We enter the store, and immediately recognize the twenty-three year-old behind the counter. The mullet is even more horrendous in person. It's abundantly clear from the expression on his face that customers from out-of-town aren't exactly a common occurrence for this establishment.

"Can I help yeh ladies with anythin'?" he asks.

"Oh, no thank you, sugar, we're just here to look around," Mary Sue says, her drawl thick as syrup. "We were passing through town on a road trip, stopped for lunch, and then decided to see what else was around to look at."

"Bit off the highway for yeh to have stumbled in on us," John says, unable to hide the suspicion in his voice.

"Yes, well, when we saw the sign on the 40 for a town called 'Bucksnort,' we just couldn't resist taking a look around and exploring, sugar," Mary Sue replies. As usual, I'm more than happy to let her do the talking.

Despite himself, John rolls his eyes, clearly not impressed by our cavalier attitude toward his hometown. Whatever, we're here to spy on and eventually kill him, not to impress him.

"Okay," he says. "Lemme know if y'all need anything, ya hear?"

"Of course, sugar, thank you for your hospitality."

Unfortunately, the shop is so tiny it doesn't take long for us to browse the inventory. Within twenty minutes, we are pushing the point where if we stay in the store any longer we will be even more conspicuous than we already have been.

For the sake of maintaining our cover of innocent patrons, Mary Sue picks a Keith Urban album off the shelf. Not really interested in any of the musical selection offered, I grab a CD at random, without even looking at what it is, and we head to the counter to checkout. While John, a look of utter boredom on his face, rings up our CD's, I surreptitiously slip a microphone bug under the lip of the counter. I have about as much hope of getting anything useful out of surveying this hole in the wall as I do for our surveying the diner where Becky Grobe works, but we should try, either way, just in case.

Our welcome in the CD store over-extended, we return to our car, and pull out onto the road. We drive down a couple blocks, then park at a location where we can keep an eye on the CD shop, without hopefully being too conspicuous from within the shop.

This day of surveillance proves to be just as exciting as the day we spent watching Clark Sr. and Becky Grobe at the diner—although that day at least ended with a more interesting turn of events, what with the mysterious town hall meeting and all. Today, when four o'clock rolls along, John passes the store off to the evening shift and leaves. We debate following him to see where he goes, but as we both have dates for tonight, we decide we'd better get back to the hotel to prepare.

As with last night, Mary Sue heads out for her date

around six, and I head over to the Buckstar on the corner for my date at seven. This time, even though I again arrived a few minutes early, I find Duke already waiting. Nanetta is pleasantly surprised by this, and Sarah desperately wants to cause Nanetta a long and painful death.

The date goes, if possible, even better than the first one. We don't really talk about anything in particular—we just talk. And talk. I start to wonder if somehow Mary Sue has possessed me, because I am finding Nanetta actually *likes* talking. To Duke, at least. Porcupines, if you *ever* tell this to Mary Sue, I swear by my pretty floral bonnet I will pull myself out of the pages of this book—*a la* that creepy chick from *The Ring*—and rip your throat out. You have been warned.

When the date comes to an end, we hug again, and this time he kisses me on the cheek—and now more than Nanetta's stomach is fluttering. I know no matter how much I try, I won't be able to hide this from Mary Sue, and she is going to be absolutely unbearable.

Duke and I agree to hold off on meeting again tomorrow night, but settle on having a third date on Saturday. As we part into the night, Nanetta finds herself wondering how she will be able to go forty-eight hours without seeing Duke, and Sarah finds herself wondering what the fuck is wrong with this Nanetta person, anyway.

Shortly after getting back to my room, I get a phone call from Mary Sue.

"Hey hon, it's me," she says. "I'm almost back to the hotel. Can you do me a favor and order up some room service? I don't care what, just as long as it's heavy on the alcohol. I'm gonna need some serious liquor before bed tonight."

"Sure thing. See you soon."

"Oh God, you're falling in love with the guy, aren't you? Nanetta, this ain't gonna end well."

"Where the fuck did you get *that* from?"

"I can hear it in your voice. Well, that and the fact you didn't throw any sarcastic quips at me about my needing to cut back on the alcohol."

"Bitch, you don't know what you're talking about."

"Whatever you say, darlin'. See you in like five minutes."

"Fine."

I hang up the phone with all the anger my thumb on a button can muster (it's times like these when I realize how inadequate modern cell phones are compared to the traditional land line phone you could slam down with all the aplomb of a 1950's movie diva), then call room service and order a couple bottles of bourbon. Two bottles is probably more than we'll need, I admit, but when it comes to alcohol my philosophy is it's better to have more than you need than not enough.

A few minutes later, a knock comes at my door, and I let Mary Sue into the room.

"Oh. My. God, Nanetta, I honestly don't know how I'm going to go through with this. The guy is a total loser, and even worse he's boring as *fuck*."

Before I can muster a response to her tirade, I am saved by another knock at the door.

"That'll be the room service," I say, returning back to the door.

The room service waiter graciously enters and

places the two bottles of bourbon on the desktop. I sign for the check, leaving the waiter a generous tip on the tab of T.H.E.M., and then turn my back to him so Mary Sue and I can continue our conversation as he leaves.

The next few seconds pass in a blur of confusion. Mary Sue's eyes open wide as saucers, she yells, "Sarah, duck!" (The fact she slipped and used my real name somehow triggers my natural reflexes to follow her order without question). Next thing I know, a knife is flying out of Mary Sue's hand and over my quickly ducking head—if she weren't a T.H.E.M. operative, I might wonder where the knife came from, but one of the things T.H.E.M. trains all of its operatives to do, especially *ass*assins, is how to cleverly conceal weapons for quick and easy retrieval. I hear a wet, squishy *thunk* behind me, and spin around in my squatting position to see Mary Sue's knife firmly planted in the left eye of the waiter, who has a handgun aimed at where the back of my head had been moments before.

The waiter drops the gun without firing and then promptly collapses to the floor of my room.

19

"**WHAT THE *ACTUAL FUCK?*"** I ask, of no one in particular.

Mary Sue, who did not just have a gun pointed at the back of her head, pulls herself together faster than I do. While I'm still processing what just happened, she's already off the bed, across the room closing the door, and dialing Zeke on her cell phone.

"Zeke, we have a problem," she says once the door is closed. "The room service waiter just tried to kill us."

I can just imagine Zeke's incredulous response to *that* statement.

"Yeah . . . Yeah . . . Okay, you got it boss," and then she hangs up. Zeke is nothing if not efficient. "He's going to dispatch an extraction team, but it will have to wait until tomorrow. By the time the team would arrive if he sent them right away, it would be the middle of the night and they'd be way more conspicuous waltzing through the lobby at that time. In the meantime, I suggest we relocate to my room for the night and you can bunk up on the pull-out sofa in my room."

Look. As you should have figured out by now, I ain't exactly a 'delicate flower' who will fall apart at the first sign of trauma and need to have a sleepover with my girlfriend in order to get through the night. *However,* if I don't have to sleep in the same room with the corpse of a man who just tried to shoot me in the back of the head, I'm not going to. So yes, I accept Mary Sue's offer.

"Is he going to relocate us to another hotel?" I ask, though I can guess the answer. I know Zeke's mind way too well for comfort.

"No. That would be even more conspicuous. In the morning, the extraction team will dispose of the body, clean up the mess before housekeeping sees it, and the hotel will stay in the dark as to what just happened. They'll have to assume this douche bag just walked off the job in the middle of his shift, or something."

I quickly gather a few things together (along with the two bottles of bourbon) to get me through the night, and as we are preparing to move our operation over to Mary Sue's room next door, I stop and say, "Wait, one more thing."

I go over to the collapsed waiter and turn his body over so I can read his name tag: Craig. I then go to my in-room phone, call the room service extension and tell the operator, "Hi, this is Nanetta Dieterle in room 1236, I just wanted to pay a compliment to the waiter, Craig. He was just exceptionally polite and friendly, and I thought his manager should know he's got himself a real keeper, with that one."

The operator thanks me and says she'll be sure to let Craig's supervisor know about my compliment.

"Good thinking," Mary Sue says, after I've hung up. "Now they won't come looking for him here. At least not for a while."

"Exactly. This ain't my first ro-day-o, cowgirl."

Even with my southern accent, it comes out sounding sarcastic, somehow.

As we move next door—placing the Do Not Disturb sign on my door to keep the housekeepers at bay until the extraction team arrives in the morning—I take a quick surveillance of the floor's hallway and notice two security cameras at either end of the hall. Once inside Mary Sue's room, I send Zeke a text message: "Security camera surveillance on the floors," knowing he'll know what to do. Within minutes, T.H.E.M.'s I.T. department will have hacked the hotel's security footage and they'll be able to edit it to show Craig arriving at our room, and then shortly departing thereafter. Hopefully by the time they realize Craig is missing, the edit will be complete.

"Okay, so what the fuck just happened?" I ask.

"I'm guessing 'Craig' is one of the T.H.E.M. operatives who accepted Nick's offer and defected," Mary Sue replies easily. Obviously, I'd guessed as much myself, but sometimes I must admit it's good to talk things out. Sometimes.

"Or it could have even been Nick, himself," I suggest, though I know it's probably a long-shot.

"Doubt it," Mary Sue replies, confirming my own doubt. "Now he has minions working for him, he'll probably be off somewhere pulling the strings and delegating rather than getting into the mess himself."

"Fuck. And this won't be the end of it. That jizz-basket Howard said most of the hotel's staff is new—for all we know half the staff could be T.H.E.M. defectors."

"Hang on with the doomsday prophecies, Little

Miss Hyperbole," Mary Sue admonishes. "As far as we know, Nick has only so far recruited four operatives to his cause. Now he's down to three. So that's far from 'half the staff.' Also, let's look at the fact that unless Nick somehow found out about our mission *at least* a few weeks before Zeke even assigned it to us, there can't be that many of his operatives positioned on the hotel staff."

"Okay, okay. But you know what I mean."

"Yeah, I do. We'll just have to be on guard going forward. Clearly Nick and his cohorts are aware of our mission, and know where we are."

"For fuck's sake, *how* is Nick doing this? How is he staying a step ahead of us at every fucking turn?"

"We don't know how far ahead he is. For all we know, 'Craig' might have only been hired within the last couple days. If the hotel *just* re-opened, it's possible. Also, you said Nick's able to disguise himself without the help of the Makeover Specialists. Maybe once he confirmed where we were assigned, he moved in, killed the 'real' Craig and then made over one of his minions to look like Craig. If he can do it to himself, it should be even easier to do it to other people. Hell, if he can make himself into a passing resemblance of David Brennan, then making one of his minions to look like Craig the Waiter would probably be a piece of arsenic-flavored cake."

I bite my lip, considering this point. "Okay, you're probably right about all of that. I still can't help feeling like Nick has got some sort of heeby jeebie voodoo working here . . . and you know I don't believe in any of that shit, but damn it . . . "

Mary Sue sighs and says, "I know. But we can

speculate until we turn blue in the face. We accepted this assignment so we could get answers, and it looks like we're on track to getting those answers. Nick knows we are here and he is already trying to get at us, so we must be doing something right. We just need to stay frosty and be ready for the next person to come at us."

"Good on that," I reply. "So, what's our next step?"

"First, we are going to have our way with those bottles of bourbon, and then I suggest we wind down and call it a night. We will have a big day tomorrow, what with the extraction team, stalking the Andersons, and fighting off rogue hospitality employees."

Despite myself, I laugh. Porcupines, I hate how Mary Sue grows on me.

"Deal," I respond.

While we drink, Mary Sue talks about her date with the groping wonder, Clark Jr. She gets so wrapped up in dissing the skeeze, she completely forgets to ask about my date with Duke, which I'm grateful for.

Before we realize it, we've gone through the first bottle and half of the second.

"Shit . . . fast that went," Mary Sue hiccups.

"You know you talk like Yoda when you're drunk, don't you?"

"Strong with the bourbon, I be."

She then breaks into a hysterical fit of giggles. I role my eyes, and leave her to her giggles so I can take a shower, hoping to wash away some of the tension lingering from almost being shot by the waiter. It proves to be a mostly futile exercise, but I do feel a bit better by the end of it. By the time I've finished, Mary Sue's finished giggling and we swap places—while she showers, I begin making up the pull-out sofa.

As I settle in, Mary Sue emerges from the bathroom wearing a long, white nightgown and carrying three grapes and an onion. I watch, perplexed, as she crosses to her bed and proceeds to peel the grapes and onion, throwing each shred into the bedside trashcan as she does so.

"What in the name of Michal Fassbender's beautiful penis are you doing?" I ask her.

"It's my anti-inflammatory nightly peel," Mary Sue responds casually, as if this is the most obvious answer in the world.

When there's nothing left to peel, she reaches into her nightstand, pulls out an old toothbrush and begins brushing her hair (yes . . . her hair . . . with a *toothbrush).* As she brushes, she softly sings:

> *Bim bam beieren*
> *Zeg ken jij de mosselman*
> *Zie je de kastanjesaan de bomen*
> *Foekepotterij, foekepotterij*
> *Duimelot is in het water gevallen*
> *Elsje Fiederelsjezetzeklompjesbij 't vuur*
> *Herfst, herfst, watheb je tekoop*
> *Boer watzeg je van mijnkippen*
> *De bezem, de bezem*
> *Maantje, maantje*

Considering the explanation I received for inquiring about her 'nightly peel,' I refrain from asking about this bizarre ritual. I don't want to know. I *really* don't want to know.

When she comes to the end of her Dutch lullaby, I hope—futilely –this is the end and I will *at last* be able to go to sleep and put this unworldly experience of sharing a room with Mary Sue far, *far* behind me.

Alas, my torture is not yet over, for Mary Sue jumps up and flips into a head stand—her nightgown falling down over her head leaving me to see everyone nature (well, with some help of the F.U.C.K.'s) gave her—her legs scissoring back and forth in the air as she balances upside down and hums *Row, Row, Row Your Boat*. I squeeze my eyes shut, trying not to scream, and keep them shut even after I hear the slight thump, indicating Mary Sue has returned to an upright position.

When I at last feel brave enough to open my eyes, I see Mary Sue has changed into a set of flannel footie P.J.'s and is *finally* settling into bed.

At the sight of the full-body P.J.'s, I lose my cool and snap, "Why the fuck were you wearing the nightgown for your aerobics, if you were just going to change into Dennis the Menace pajamas anyway?"

"Footies are too restrictive for my circulation exercises," Mary Sue responds, apparently oblivious to my indignation. "And it's not like I could *possibly* do my exercises nude—that would be totally rude and inappropriate. Duh."

I roll my eyes with much aggravation, and sigh, "Whatever. Let's just get some sleep, please."

"Sure thing, girlfriend! G'night, grumpy-pants!"

With a click, the lights are off and I think at last I have a reprieve. Another click, and the T.V. lights up and the sounds of *Alexandra Cameltoe* fill the room. I silently groan, then concede it could be worse. Eventually, I am able to drift off to the song *Right Hand Job*.

20

AGAIN THE DREAMS haunt my night, and again the only change is Duke has taken Jason's place in the cycle. I wake up, every muscle in my body feeling knotted and tense, a little before eight. Mary Sue, I see, is already up, dressed, and about.

"Mornin' sleepy head," she chirps cheerfully, making me want to take her grape and onion peels from the night before and shove them down her cheerful throat. "You must've been having some dream there, I couldn't tell if you were having the time of your life or being chased by Freddy Krueger."

"I think I would've preferred the torments of Krueger," I respond, rubbing the sleep from my eyes, and if Mary Sue thinks I am going to say anything more than *that* on the subject of my dreams, she is going to be sorely mistaken.

"Just got a text from Zeke," Mary Sue says, mercifully changing course. "The extraction team will be arriving in a couple hours. We will need to be here when they arrive."

"Great, so we're stuck here until then," I groan. I don't like being placed under house arrest.

"Time'll fly, you'll see. Let's start off with getting some breakfast."

"Fine, but no room service."

"Agreed."

"And then I'm going to need another trip to the spa."

"How'd I guess?"

Whatever. After the night I just had—first almost getting killed by a waiter, Mary Sue's nightly ablutions, and then the return of my cycle of dreams—I certainly cannot be expected to function without some pampering first.

We make our way down to the hotel restaurant on the first floor. Every employee we cross paths with, I now find myself eyeing suspiciously, wondering if they might be another minion of Nick Jin's in disguise.

After breakfast, I go to the spa to make a walk-in appointment, and Mary Sue returns to her room. The spa isn't too busy this morning, so I have practically no wait at all and am able to request my buddy, Bill, who has returned from his day off.

After my massage, I return to Mary Sue's room, and almost as soon as I walk through her door, there comes a simultaneous *ding* from both of our cell phones, signaling a message from Zeke: *The team is at your hotel.*

We step out of Mary Sue's room and move next door to mine, so we can be there when the extraction team arrives. I half-expect to find Craig the Waiter's body missing when we return to the room, but his corpse lies right where we left it the night before.

Barely a minute later, a knock comes at the door and I open it to find two inconspicuous, blond-haired, blue-eyed, business-suited men with briefcases waiting outside the door. Without a word, the two men enter the room and I close the door behind them. Sometimes a larger extraction team will be sent, but as we are in a hotel, Zeke no doubt decided a team of two would draw less attention—it will be easy enough to claim these two Yuppy Aryans are lawyers here to discuss the case we are working on.

The Yuppy Aryans wordlessly cross the room to my bed and lay down their briefcases. Yuppy Aryan Number One turns to me and Mary Sue and says, "You two may continue with whatever work you need to. We won't be long."

Yuppy Aryan Number One then nods to Yuppy Aryan Number Two and they proceed with their work. Mary Sue and I have both seen this whole process before, so I'll just lay out a general summary for you.

The Yuppy Aryan Twins will remove enough tools from their two briefcases to convince you the cases are magically enhanced, or something. First thing they'll do is lay out a large clear sheet of plastic and roll the corpse onto the sheet. They will then proceed with dismantling the body, piece-by-piece. Each piece they dismantle will get placed into one of those vacuum-suck-storage-bag things, only these bags compress *way* more than the ones you can buy off of infomercials. Basically, you put an average-sized foot into the bag, and once the compression is done it's the size of a tennis ball. Each compression makes a delightfully disgusting *squish-crunch-fwoosh* noise as the high-powered vacuum squeezes air, bone, and fleshy matter. Morbidly neato tech, if you ask me.

They proceed piece-by-piece, until the entire body

is contained in tiny bags which can easily be placed inside the two suitcases and carried off to a T.H.E.M. facility for final disposal. Once they've finished dismantling, they roll the tarp back up (which has, naturally, gotten messy in this process), and place it in a vacuum bag as well.

The last thing the extraction team is responsible for before calling it a day is cleaning up any evidence left behind—such as the substantial pool of dried blood which formed on the carpet after Mary Sue's knife made a nest for itself in Craig the Waiter's eye socket.

When a full extraction team is sent, this process can take as little as twenty minutes to complete. However, with only two extractors it takes closer to forty-five minutes. But still, not bad timing to dispose of an entire body with no trace what-so-ever.

Since we don't have much work to do, we decide to watch T.V. while the Yuppy Aryan Twins do their thing. Ironically, *Saw* is showing.

Almost as soon as the Yuppy Aryan Twins finish packing up and leave, my room phone rings. Mary Sue and I exchange an ominous look before I pick it up.

"Good morning Miss Dieterle, I'm sorry to disturb you, but I'm glad you are still here this morning. My name is Charles Dillon, the hotel's General Manager, and I'm afraid I have an urgent matter to discuss with you."

Obviously I know what this is going to be about, but I have to play dumb.

"Oh dear, I hope my company's credit card hasn't declined or anything . . . "

"No, no. Nothing like that," Mr. Dillon assures me. "It's actually about one of our employees, Craig."

"Oh, yes, Craig! He delivered our drinks last night. Lovely boy—I'd called after he left and gave the operator a compliment to deliver to his manager. Is that what this is about?"

"No . . . well, not really."

Knowing what Mr. Dillon is *trying* to get to, while he pussyfoots around the matter, is simply agonizing. But, like I said, I can't let on I already know, and so I wait for him to get there himself.

"You see," Mr. Dillon proceeds, "after Craig delivered your drinks last night he . . . well, he must have walked off the job, because no one saw him after that."

"Really?" I say, putting all the fake shock into my voice I can muster. Meryl Streep, eat your mother-fucking heart out, bitch. "That's so strange!"

"Yes, we thought so, too. It was only his second day on the job—it wouldn't be exactly unheard of for someone to quit so soon after starting like that, but to just walk off in the middle of the shift without saying anything to anyone, that's very odd. We got the message about your compliment of his service, so we just wanted to see if there was anything odd about his behavior when you saw him, because it seems you were the last person to have seen him."

"Odd? Goodness, no! He was absolutely lovely. I mean, it was only an order of two bottles of bourbon, so I wouldn't have blamed him if he wasn't on top of his form for us, but he was the consummate professional and super friendly; he asked about what brought us into the area, and how our evening was going, and just very engaging. That's why he stood out to me and I wanted to make sure he got credit where credit is deserved."

"Since nobody saw him after he left your room, we don't know how you paid for the bottles of bourbon. Did you maybe pay cash? Just wondering if perhaps he took the cash and ran. That might explain his unexplained disappearance."

"No, I charged it to our room tab—even the tip, so the only thing he had to run off with from me was my signature. Goodness, I hope nothing has happened to him!"

"Myself as well, Ms. Dieterle. Thank you for the information, it has been very helpful. I'm sure it won't come to this —we'll probably find out he just decided, for whatever, reason the job wasn't for him and wanted to avoid confrontation—but if we do have to get the police involved if Craig does not turn up anywhere, can I count on you to give your testimony to the police as well?"

In my pre-T.H.E.M. days, such a question probably would have sent me screaming for the eyed hills. But now, I laugh at the idea of being scared of the fuzz. The po-po just fo' show and ain't no foe, yo. Yeah . . . I can't talk gangsta. Sorry for that.

"Of course," I respond, "anything I can do to help figure out what happened, I'd be more than willing to assist with, Mr. Dillon."

"Thank you, Ms. Dieterle. Sorry for disturbing your time, if there's anything else we can do for you, please let us know."

"Thank you, Mr. Dillon, have yourself a good day now, ya hear?"

"So I take it they've noticed Craig the Waiter's gone missing?" Mary Sue inquires once I've hung up the phone on Mr. Dillon.

"Yep. And you were right—he'd just started working. Yesterday was his second day."

"Well, that was easy. Sucks for the hotel and the cops though, 'cause that means not only did our Extraction Team completely get rid of the body and evidence, but it also means until a few days ago 'Craig' probably didn't even exist at all. They'll be chasing their fucking tails for days trying to find him."

"Indeed. Anyway, it's nearly noon now. Should we go ahead with our original plan of getting down to Bucksnort and tailing Bobby Anderson for the day?"

"Will we have time to even make it worthwhile? I mean, we'll have to come back first to get ready for our dates again."

"What are you talking about? I'm not seeing Duke tonight. We decided to hold off a night and go out again tomorrow night instead."

"What? Why didn't *I* think of that?" Mary Sue yells in disgust, though whether she's more disgusted with me or herself, I can't say.

"I don't know," I respond, smiling sadistically. "Clearly you just lack my dating finesse."

"Fuck, fuck, fuck, fuck, fuck!"

"Language!"

I won't lie, I enjoy these moments when the tables are turned for us. I love seeing Mary Sue unravel and I get to be the calm one sarcastically jabbing at her meltdown.

"God damn it. And this is going to be the third date, too . . . " Mary Sue is now pacing across the hotel room, fury pouring from every pore.

"So? What does that have to do with anything?"

"It's the *third* date. Don't tell me you don't know what that means."

"You're getting ice cream?"

"Jeez, Sar—sorry, Nanetta. You really have lived under a dating rock your whole life, haven't you?"

"Pretty much."

"The third date is the one where usually you . . . ya know . . . do the *horizontal hula* . . . "

"That's stupid."

Granted, there's only been two guys who I've been on more than three dates with. The first one was my high school boyfriend, and I killed him before we got up to any of that hanky panky stuff. The second was Jason, who I banged on the first date and it was the fact that for some reason I didn't have any temptation to kill him afterward which had me continue to date him.

"Well, it's not a *law* or anything," Mary Sue says, as she continues to pace. "If I was just dating Clark Jr. for the fun of dating, I could let it happen naturally. But I'm not dating him for the fun of dating—God, I can't imagine any woman pathetic enough to date him for the fun of it. I can't risk him losing patience and walking away—we need the intel."

"Sounds like you've got quite the predicament." She ignores me.

"So basically, if he makes a move tonight—and of course this loser will, he's been making moves since our first date—I'm gonna have to give in, for the sake of the mission."

"You are the model of feminism."

"Oh shut up. You've got it easy. At least your mark isn't a total dipshit."

She has a point, so I decide to stop teasing her.

"Okay, so fair enough. But still, we need to figure out what we're going to do for the rest of the day. Are we going to lose this entire day, just because you're dreading putting out tonight?"

Mary Sue at last stops pacing and plops down on the bed.

"No, we don't want to throw our entire day away," Mary Sue sighed with exasperation. "But I don't think it's practical to drive back and forth to Bucksnort all those times, just for maybe a couple hours' worth of surveillance."

"Fair enough. So what do you suggest?"

"We haven't gotten in any martial arts practice since we got here. What ya say we find a park somewhere nearby and get some practice in?"

"Sounds like a plan, my sister from a diff'rent mister! To the Skank Mobile!"

Mary Sue shoots me a look of utter loathing, and snaps, "I thought we weren't calling it that?"

"It's growing on me," I reply with a wicked smile.

I suppose on some level I should feel guilty for enjoying torturing Mary Sue so much right now, but then I remember everything she put me through last night, and my guilt disappears. Karma is a bitch, but she's a beautiful bitch, and she's *my* bitch.

21

BACK WHEN MARY SUE first approached me and suggested she give me some martial arts lessons, I naturally assumed it would entail washing her car and other tedious chores that would later grow into my becoming an instantaneous award-winning karate champion, after a motivational montage or two, underscored by an instant-chart topping '80's pop-rock tune.

So, I was kind of disappointed to find training—with Mary Sue, at least—was nothing like the movies. She never made me wash her car even once. With Mary Sue, my training was more a series of alternating between attacking her, and defending myself from her. In the beginning, regardless of whether I was on the offense or defense, I always ended up flat on my back with my breath knocked out of me. Now, it's more like five out of ten times I end up getting my ass whopped by the buxom Barbie, so yay for improvement.

We find a park on the outskirts of Dickson which appears to be fairly remote and unpopulated. Even though our training isn't necessarily anything nefarious or suspicious, we still would prefer to keep it under the radar and not risk it compromising our covers for the job.

When we'd first started training, Mary Sue would stop after kicking my ass and point out what I'd done wrong. We've pretty much moved past that, and now just come at each other with our best respective fight until one of us is knocked out. I've gotten to the point where I can analyze my own attack and see what I could have done better without her pointing it out to me.

I don't know if it's because we haven't had any practice sessions in a while, or if Mary Sue is just extra riled up about her dreaded third date with Clark Jr., but she really beats the crap out of me today. For the sake of my own ego, I am going to go with the theory she's taking out her extra aggravation, and not that I've lost that much traction. I do get a couple wins in, but for the most part Mary Sue dominates the scoreboard today.

You might think spending an entire afternoon beating the snot out of one another would damage our friendship or, at least, leave us exhausted, but just the opposite. Fighting actually strengthens the bond between us—for me, having the opportunity to act on the violent tendencies Mary Sue often inspires in me is some sort of venting catalyst—and by the end of our session, I'm invigorated, re-energized. I feel like fighting Mary Sue has allowed me to unleash many of the demons I've been carrying on my back for the last few days. It's not as therapeutic as actually killing someone, but it's a close second.

Our training/battle session is brought to an end when, in the late afternoon, the overhead sky turns grey and ominous with the threat of approaching rain. Indeed, by the time we make it back to the hotel the threat of rain has manifested into a virtual monsoon.

As we dash out of our car toward the hotel, we are greeted halfway by Tim the Bellman with an umbrella. As he escorts us into the dry sanctuary of the lobby, we can't help but notice a kerfuffle at the registration desk. A large, rotund, balding, and evidently intoxicated gentleman is screaming at the poor clerk behind the desk.

"I don't care about any of that," the behemoth screams, "my balcony is soaking wet and I want someone to come up and try it *now!*"

"But sir . . . it's still raining right now . . . " the poor clerk stammers.

"I don't give a flying rat's ass if it's raining. I paid good money for this room, and I want a dry balcony, so you had better make that happen, or I'll have your job, you hear me?"

Nanetta would probably just keep walking at this point, feeling bad for the poor clerk, but not wanting to get involved. I've given Nanetta enough wins over the last few days while dating Duke that I'm more than willing to let Sarah take over this time, damn the consequences.

"Excuse me," I say in my sweetest belle accent, stepping up to the desk and confronting the walrus-man, "but perhaps I can explain this situation to you better. You see that stuff coming down from the sky out there? That's called 'rain.' Rain is made of water. Water is wet. So rain makes things wet. Therefore, even if this poor gentleman were able to send up someone to dry up your balcony for you, it would just get wet again by the time they were done. Do you understand, or should I use smaller words?"

I don't know which makes me happier—the look of gratitude from the poor desk clerk, or the look of utter stupefaction from Captain Weather. It seems people calling him out on his bullshit is not something he's entirely used to.

After a few moments, he regains himself and replies, "Listen sweetheart," (mistake number one: *don't* call me sweetheart), "why don't you mind yer own bus'ness and go powder yer nose or somethin'." (Mistake number two: being a condescending, misogynistic asshole).

I might have let him get away with strikes one and two, but when he went for the grand third strike of trying to smack my ass—well, anyone who knows me probably wouldn't be surprised to learn Captain Weather's hand never made it to my ass.

Next thing he knows, Captain Weather is on the ground, the hand guilty of attempted butt-smacking twisted behind him, and my knee on his throat. He seems to be sputtering something about a lawsuit or something, but I prcss my knee on his esophagus harder, and that does the job of shutting him up. I may not have been able to take on the Queen of Jiu Jitsu, today, but Captain Weather is no match for me.

"No, why don't *you* listen here, sweetheart," I reply, my voice quiet but deadly. "You were being very rude to this poor hotel worker, and then you were very rude to me. I will gladly forget both of these offenses if you agree to shut your ass up, go back to your room, and leave the poor staff of this hotel alone until you've sobered up. Blink twice if you comprehend what I'm telling you, once if you need smaller words."

The purpling man blinks twice frantically, and I release my hold on him. Tim the Bellman rushes over to help Captain Weather up. For a moment, it seems like he is about to fire off another retort, but I take a single menacing step towards him, and he reluctantly thinks twice.

As Tim the Bellman leads the sputtering Captain Weather toward the elevator, the clerk behind the desk whispers sheepishly at me, "That was the most amazing thing I have ever seen . . . thank you."

"Anytime, sugar," I say with a wink, and then make my way back to Mary Sue.

"So much for keeping a low profile," Mary Sue whispers as we make our way toward the elevators.

"Oh, whatever. That asshole had it coming."

"Don't get me wrong, I'm not saying it wasn't brilliant, all I'm saying is a bit of a 'character break' for Nanetta, don't ya think?"

"Meh. So she's taken some self defense classes, and sticks her neck out for 'the little guy' from time-to-time. Doesn't give anyone any reason to link her to a psychopathic serial killer."

"Fair enough," Mary Sue says with a shrug, as we step into the elevator.

When we arrive at the twelfth floor, we find Tim the Bellman waiting for the elevator. As we step out so he can step in, he looks around quickly to make sure no one can hear him, then whispers to me, "I just wanted to say, Miss Dieterle, that was *amazing*. Mr. Crowley has been absolutely horrid to the staff ever since he checked in. I have a feeling the rest of the staff will be talking about you tackling that asshole for a while."

"Glad to have been of service, Tim," I say with a smile, as the elevator doors close, separating us. Then a realization hits me, and I say, "Fuck."

"What?" Mary Sue asks, confused about my sudden turn of attitude.

"Tim was bringing that asshole back to his room . . . which means he's on this floor—our floor. We might run into him again."

"I wouldn't worry about it. After that ass-kicking he just got, I'm sure he won't be giving you any trouble—assuming he even remembers anything once he sobers up."

"Fair enough," I say with a shrug. I'm certainly not scared of having another run-in with Captain Weather—or *Mr. Crowley*, as Tim the Bellman called him—I'd just rather not if I don't have to.

We part at our rooms, and Mary Sue goes to get ready for her date, leaving me to decide what to do with myself for the rest of the night. I decide to settle for a long bath followed by a marathon binge of *Mister What* episodes—my guilty relaxation pleasure. Unfortunately, ever since Nick impersonated David Brennan to get into my pants in Duluth, that has somewhat ruined my appreciation for my former favorite Mister. As such, I skip over the David Brennan seasons and go to his replacement, Matthew Smytheson. Smytheson, though endearing, is no competition for David Brennan, but seeing as I can't look at David anymore without thinking of Nick, Smytheson will have to do. Nick has even managed to ruin *Mister What* for me, the fucking bastard.

It is nearly midnight, and I am on the verge of falling asleep watching *Mister What*, when an insistent knock pounds at my door.

Grumbling at having been stolen away from unconsciousness, I climb out of bed, pull on my bathrobe, and make my way to the door. I open it to find Mary Sue waiting anxiously in the hallway—she pushes her way into my room, muttering, "We need to talk."

"Jesus Christ," I respond, closing the door behind me, "surely even Clark Jr. couldn't have been so bad that this can't wait until morning . . . "

"What? Oh, God. No. I mean, yes . . . it was . . . no, I can't talk about that now. I'm not here about that. It's . . . you haven't been out of your room, have you?"

"Not since we got back, no. I've been holed up in here. Why?"

"And no one's called or come to talk to you or anything?"

"No . . . why would they?"

Mary Sue's ambiguity is truly driving me mad right now.

"Nanetta," she says, and I can tell we're about to finally get to the point of all of this, "it's Mr. Crowley. The asshole from the lobby earlier. He was murdered just down in his room, 1208."

22

GUESS I don't need to tell you this is bad. I don't mean that Fuck-tard the Wonder Weatherman go axed. Hell, that's pretty fucking brilliant, if you ask me. There is nothing in the universe more beautiful than witnessing Karma in action.

However, as far as the mission goes, this is an unfortunate complication—which is not made easier by the fact I was one of the last people seen to interact with the victim, and that was not exactly the most amiable of conversations.

And then of course is the fact this is most likely the work of Nick and his cronies, meaning there's at least one more T.H.E.M. turncoat working or staying at the hotel. I don't like complications, and just like Duluth this mission is turning into a clusterfuck of complications.

I won't bore you with the details, but the rest of the night and most of the next morning is spent being interrogated by the cops. Needless to say, it has also surfaced I was the last person to see Craig the Waiter disappear, so now his sudden vanishing has piqued the pigs' interest, as well. Fucking a'.

Fortunately, this is not my first time at this game.

I didn't kill thirteen people without getting caught to let a thing like this slip me up. I put on my best innocent little flower act, and even Sherlock Fucking Holmes wouldn't suspect me.

Nevertheless, after the cops are finally done interrogating me, I get a call from Zeke chewing me out. Basic summary of Zeke's general point: I am a fucking moron for being so stupid as to risk my cover by tangling with Captain Weather. Surprisingly enough, I had already figured all of that out on my own, but thanks for making me feel like even more of a shithead, Zeke. Asshole.

By the time I'm done getting yelled at by Zeke, I realize it's almost noon, I have a date in seven hours, and I've gotten almost no sleep. I consider cancelling with Duke, but I don't want to risk setting back the mission (well . . . that's what I tell myself and Mary Sue, at least . . . but if I'm going to be honest, I admit Nanetta *really* needs to see Duke after the night she/I/we just had).

I book a quickie walk-in massage with my favorite masseuse, Bill, and then retire for a mid-afternoon nap before my date.

You would think with all the extra stress and excitement, I might be too exhausted to dream, but alas. Every sleeping-moment is plagued by my now-usual cycle of dreams (I had the same result in the few-hour reprieve I had between the midnight and early-morning police interrogations).

At five, I get up and take a bath before getting ready. For some reason I can't quite identify, my stomach is a knot of tension as I prepare for tonight's date with Duke. Naturally, it's Mary Sue who brings on the eventual epiphany, when I run into her on my way out of the hotel.

"So, you ready for tonight?" she says with a coy wink.

"What are you on about?" I sigh, too tired to read through her cryptic girl chat.

"It's *the third date*, silly. We covered this already, remember? God knows you've got a better chance than I did at having a good time. Hell, it was already over before I even had a chance to fake an orgasm."

As usual, Mary Sue has hit the nail on the head, as far as getting right to what was troubling my subconscious before even myself. Granted, I admit I'm not exactly the most introspective mother-fucker in the universe, so being a step ahead of me in the inner-psychology department is not that hard. Nonetheless, I'll be a purple monkey in Hell before I ever consider admitting that to her.

"Bitch, please," I say, rolling my eyes in the hope of affecting a guise of complete disregard for her theory. "Just because you felt the need to conform to a ridiculous misogynistic dating dogma with a lowlife hillbilly who probably thinks the clitoris is in your belly button, doesn't mean I'm going to put-out just because it's my third date."

"Sheesh, bite my head off why don't you," Mary Sue bites back, hurt. "Granted, your absolutely right about the belly clit, but still. God, that was fucking awkward . . ."

"I'm sorry. It's been a long day." I hate to admit I mean the apology.

"It's okay," she responds. As usual, Mary Sue is as forgiving as a golden fucking retriever. "Look, try not to think about any of that. Just have a good time tonight—with or without the sex, you've earned a break."

"I won't argue that," I say with a sigh.

She hugs me goodbye, something I normally would not welcome, even or especially from Mary Sue, but either I'm too tired to push her away or I'm getting used to her affections. We'll go with me being tired.

With every step from the hotel to the Buckstars, I silently tell myself I am not going to bend to Mary Sue's silly dating rules. I will superglue my pants on if that's what it takes to prove her wrong.

As soon as I walk into the Buckstars, I instantly feel the weight of all the baggage I've been carrying all day just falling away. The familiar shop has become an oasis from the reality of my world—a place where Nanetta can take over and Sarah can sit off on the sidelines.

Unfortunately, as soon as I see Duke at the back of the shop, there's one other thing that sheds away along with my stress—my conviction to resist Mary Sue's third date decree. I see him sitting in the back—at our usual table (the fact *I* have a usual table with a guy at Buckstars makes Sarah want to puke and Nanetta want to swoon)—with his hair slicked back, his beard neatly trimmed, and a nice button-down shirt and khakis . . . even Sarah melts to her core, and I know this is one battle of wills that Nanetta is going to win. It comforts me little to know my submission has nothing to do with some stupid 'three date rule' and all to do with the sheer fact that after months of brewing over Nick Jin's trickery, I just really need to get porked by someone who preferably isn't a psychopath hell bent on killing me and everyone I work with.

I will my legs not to turn into useless blobs of jelly, and try to exude an aura of calm as I make my way to our table. Duke gets up and greets me with a hug and a kiss on the cheek. He takes my coat and I take a seat—not a moment, too soon, for my legs' resolve to continue working is quickly dissolving.

We make idle chit chat for a few minutes, sipping on our coffee, but I can't really focus on the conversation, as I'm finding myself getting lost in Duke's brown eyes.

He clearly has noticed my distraction, for he says, "Are you okay, Nanny? You seem like something's wrong?"

I shake myself out of my daze, and say, "I'm sorry. Yesterday was just crazy at work and it's left me a tad out-of-sorts. And . . . " I nervously look around the coffee shop to make sure no one is in our immediate vicinity, then lean across the table and whisper in his ear, " . . . and honestly, all I want to do tonight is take you back to my room and have my way with you."

I sit back and relish the fierce blush that overcomes Duke's face. I'll tell you this: I ain't never seen a man down a frappuccino as fast as Duke downs his in the next few seconds.

I'm not going to get overly graphic here, sorry. That shit ain't my jive, yo. I gotta stop trying to talk street.

All I'll say is . . . well, let's put it this way. It was after three in the morning when we went to sleep, and considering how my last twenty-four hours went, that should tell you several things—not the least of which is that Duke clearly keeps up on his Vitamin E.

It was good. Well, mostly good. The beginning part—the 'build-up,' if you will—that was bad, but that had nothing to do with Duke. That part has always been the part which most makes me want to run a knife into my partner's gut. I found out about my weakness for foreplay the hard way—well, I guess my first boyfriend Ted was the one who found out the hard way, if I'm going to be honest. Hell, even Jason the first few times we were together, I wanted to rip his face off with my finger nails during the pre-coital groping/petting stages.

I guess that's one reason why I prefer drunken one-night stands—those kinds of guys aren't exactly big on the foreplay, which suits me just fine, as it usually means I can get through the night without cutting the douche open from groin to sternum.

Duke, being the upstanding guy he is, was all about the foreplay, and I'm probably the only woman in the world for which that is a bad thing. But, I had to admit either A) letting him know I was not exactly into this part would probably spoil the mood, or B) giving into my urges and killing him also would probably spoil the mood (not to mention Zeke would have my head for jeopardizing the mission for a second time in barely over twenty-four hours . . .)

So, I stuck it out and let him do his thing. Hell, he probably mistook my tension as pleasure, so I guess it worked out, and once we got past the foreplay and into 'the good stuff,' I didn't have to fake anything. *Anything.*

Unfortunately, the foreplay was not the worst part of the night. The worst part—and again, this was no fault of Duke's—was after we were both spent and passed out, the dreams returned. As has been pretty thoroughly established, my primary goal in engaging in this coital exercise was that I would finally be able to vanquish these dreams from my subconscious.

As such, when I wake up at half past nine, I almost burst into tears of frustration—and as I have said before, I *don't* cry. Instead, I stifle my disappointment and—just like my usual bull-headed self—decide to face my problem the only way I know how: head on with determination. I'm not going to let this one setback deter my efforts to rid myself of these dreams. Fuck no. I'm going to keep on trying until I never have another dream for the rest of my life.

Seeing as there's no better time than the present to continue my efforts, I wake-up Duke (by doing something I would not be surprised to find out to be illegal in Tennessee . . . but he doesn't seem to mind).

After we've recovered from another round (I've lost count now . . .), Duke stretches and climbs out of bed. Starting to pull on his clothes, he says, "I should oughtta get goin', Nanny, iffin' I'm gonna get to church this mornin'."

"I'd think after last night the last place you'd want to be seen is in the Lord's House," I say with a mischievous, coy smile.

Duke laughs, and says, "True. But all the more reason for me to go and make penance for my sins."

"Okay, fine," putting on my best disappointed pout. "When can I see you again?"

I seriously don't know who I am anymore. I have *never* been *that* girl, begging a guy to spend time with her.

"I gotta work early tomorrow, so probably not

tonight—'specially not if we're gonna pull an all-nighter again."

"As fun as it would be to try, I'm pretty sure both of our sets of naughty bits would probably walk out on strike if we tried to pull another all-nighter two nights in a row."

Duke laughs again, and says, "Definitely. So message me tomorrow and we'll see where we're both at?"

"Sounds like a plan," I concur.

I get out of bed and pull on a bathrobe, so I can walk him to the door. We kiss again before he leaves, and I resist the urge to pull him back into the room and continue having my way with him.

I've barely gotten back into the room after saying goodbye, when there's a knock at the door. I don't even need to look through the peephole to guess it's Mary Sue, and I'm right.

"Good Lord, girlfriend, I thought you two would never quit. You do realize your headboard shares a wall with my headboard, right?"

"You're just jealous," I say rolling my eyes.

"I won't deny it. Lucky for you, I don't need to ask you for any details, since I got the general gist of things from the banging on the wall."

"Is there a purpose for this early morning visit, or did you just come here to annoy me?"

"Oh, nothing much. Just thought you might wanna look outside the window."

I eye her skeptically, but I can guess from her tone she's not going to elaborate further, so I cross to the window and look out.

"Fuck, fuckity, fuck-fuck-fuck!" I spit out as I see a

string of police cars in the parking lot of the hotel. "What now?"

"Another murder last night," Mary Sue replies, as if she is announcing the jam on her toast was less than satisfactory this morning. "What the hell happened?"

"Asked a couple well-placed questions, all I know for sure is it apparently wasn't on our floor, as there's been zero activity up here. Needless to say, the hotel staff is in a bit of a panic."

"I bet they are," I say with a sardonic half-laugh.

"Hopefully they no longer suspect you have any involvement in this, because we *really* do not want to have to drag your alibi from last night into all of this. That could . . . complicate things for us."

"Oh, hell no. We aren't bringing Duke into this. That will absolutely fuck this mission over when we— when *I* have to kill him at the end of all this. I don't think even Zeke would be able to cover up *that* particular snag."

"Indeed not."

"So if it comes to that, you're my alibi."

"Of course! We were having a girls' night in! Ooh, we could say we were playing Cards Against Humanity!"

"Whatever. Just as long as Duke doesn't get dragged into this."

"Sure, sure. So what do we do now?"

"I'll contact Zeke and see if he can get us more details about what happened."

"And our assignment?"

"For today we'll lay low. Stay in the hotel. Tomorrow we'll go back to Bucksnort and resume surveillance until . . . "

"Lemme guess. Until your date with Duke."

"We haven't finalized it," I snap defensively. "But . . . yeah . . . "

"Damn, girl, you have fallen hard for this hillbilly, haven't you?"

"For the last time, no. Duke is nothing to me but a piece of meat I am simultaneously using for the purpose of cleansing my palate of Nick-Fucking-Jin, and getting information for our assignment before I turn him into a literal piece of meat."

Even I don't believe the words at this point. Clearly, Mary Sue doesn't either as all she says is, "Sure thing."

Ignoring her, I pull out my phone and send a text message to Zeke: "Another murder in hotel. Not sure who/where/when. Fuzz has not approached me for ?'s yet. More info?"

Less than a minute later, I get a response: "Gimme a few."

And sure enough, barely five minutes later, I get another text: "Vic = Johnson Brown. 33 male. Killed in his room, #586. Probably around 2 am. That's all I got now. Will send more when I have it."

With that out of the way, and having already agreed to lay low for the day, Mary Sue and I decide to spend the day in my room, having the 'girls' day in' we allegedly had yesterday. Thank porcupines, for once Mary Sue is smart enough not to haggle me for girl talk about Duke and Clark Jr. I really don't need that right now.

There's a *Friday the 13th* marathon playing on cable today, which is just what I need to unwind. Nothing puts me at ease and helps me forget the woes of the world like a good comedy marathon.

23

MUCH TO MY utter disappointment and annoyance, the dreams do not abate that night. There is, however, one more tiny change to the narrative of the cycle. Previously, at the part where Jason/Duke turned into Nick, it was kind of a seamless change; one second it was Jason or Duke making love to me, and then it was Nick. I thought *that* was disturbing enough. Now, as Duke and I are going at it, I take a knife, plunge it into his back. Then, without losing a beat to the thumping of our passions, Duke reaches behind himself and begins pulling his skin away from the hole I just made in his back. He pulls and pulls, and his skin stretches, until he's peeled it all off, revealing Nick underneath.

Look, as you've undoubtedly figured out by now, I ain't exactly a squeamish girl. I've watched my share of grotesque horror movies, and more often than not they just make me laugh or want to work as a consultant for Hollywood horror writers. However, *that* is some *seriously* fucked-up shit.

So it's no wonder when I wake up from that fright show, I'm in more need of a trip to the spa than ever. Bill the Hunky Masseuse does his usual magic, but even at the end I'm still not able to shake the horrific images out of my mind.

After my massage, I return to the twelfth floor and meet up with Mary Sue. We agree to head out to Bucksnort for another day of surveillance.

Something big must have gone down in the fifteen minutes since I left the spa, because the lobby is flooded with cops. I want to believe they are just following up on the murders of the last few days, but that is probably wishful thinking.

I follow Mary Sue as she makes her way over to the bell stand, where Tim the Bellman and Howard the Supervisor are nervously watching over the proceedings of the lobby.

"What's going on?" Mary Sue asks.

"I'm afraid we can't comment," Howard stiffly replies, as if this is the thousandth time he has been asked this question (and considering the activity of the last few days, it probably *is* the thousandth time he's been asked).

"Has there been another murder?" I ask, hoping they'll let something slip.

"I already told you, we cannot comment," Howard replies shortly.

However, the look of discomfort on Tim's face is all the answer I need.

Mary Sue and I exchange a glance, but it's clear we aren't going to get any information out of Howard, so we leave them alone.

We grab a couple sandwiches from the hotel gift shop to eat later while on surveillance, and head out to the parking lot. As we pull out onto the road, I send Zeke yet another text. Normally, we try not to be in contact with HQ much while on assignment, as it's easier to stay under the radar and in character if you're not constantly calling home base. However, considering the circumstances, this mission is continuing to make me break more and more standard operating procedures.

A few minutes later, as we pull onto Interstate 40, I get a response from Zeke. "Vic = Stephanie Webber. 21 female. Found in room 669, by housekeeper, 45 minutes ago. No T.O.D. estimate yet."

"Captain Hammer's nipples," I curse. "We've been on this assignment barely a week, and Nick's already running circles around us."

"You're just upset he's killing people, and you aren't," Mary Sue replies.

She's partly right. I haven't killed anyone since the senator, and let's just say that he only barely fixed my itch for blood (especially as I blacked out for the *actual* killing part . . .) However, what is really irritating is knowing Nick Jin or one of his cronies is lurking in the shadows somewhere in our hotel, randomly picking off hotel guests just to mess with me.

You know in cartoons where the light bulb suddenly turns on over a person's head? Well, if this were a cartoon, this would be that moment—only, in keeping with the tone of this story, it wouldn't necessarily be a light bulb, per se, but more likely a victim's severed scrotum shrunken and filled with tiny, various-colored glow lights. But you get the idea.

Randomly picking off hotel guests.

"For the love of Tom Hiddleston's naked ass in *Crimson Peak*, he's doing it again . . . " I whisper.

"Come again for Big Fudge?" Mary Sue asks, confused.

"Back in Duluth . . . the people Nick was killing . . . it was a code. He left a coded message telling me where to meet him."

"And you think he's doing the same thing again?"

"I'd be willing to bet my favorite killing knife on it."

"So what *is* the code? How do we crack it?"

"There were two parts of the code in Duluth. If you lined up the victims in the order they were killed, the first letter of each name spelled out my name—to get my attention. The second part was where the body was found. None of the bodies were found where they had been murdered, they'd all been transported and dumped. The first letter of each location spelled out where he wanted to meet me."

"And how did he know when you would get the message and be there?"

"Probably using the same fucking voodoo he's been using to get inside my head all along."

As soon as those words exit my mouth, a horrible possibility about my dreams enters my mind . . . but I push that thought away. I can't think about *that* now.

"So we need sit down and look at each murder and look for common threads, yes?" Mary Sue prompts, breaking me out of my meditations.

"Yes, exactly. I honestly stumbled on the code by accident, as I was trying to make sense of the murders. I listed them all out and then noticed my name was spelled out."

"Alright, well we'll do that as soon as we get back to the hotel tonight."

"Sounds good. Oh, fuck."

"What?"

"Duke. We were going to go out again."

"I thought you hadn't finalized anything?"

"Well . . . yeah . . . "

"Look, your engine can go without an oil change for a night—I heard how lubricated you got on Saturday, remember? *This* is more important than the Anderson mission, this is the *real* reason we are here."

"You're right," I admit. Truth be told, considering how I just admitted to myself a few minutes ago that I'm feeling blood lusty lately, I probably should pace myself with seeing Duke too often right now anyway, just in case I do lose control—never mind the fact that since my dreams got worse, not better, since sleeping with Duke, my hopes that healthy non-Nick copulation will make them stop are steadily dwindling.

Even so, I would be lying if I said I hadn't been looking forward to seeing him again, even with the risk of 'accidentally' killing him mid-coitus and still being stuck with infuriating sex-dream-nightmares.

"What about Clark Jr.? Did you have plans with him?"

"No, I've been pretending I'm sick, so I can put him off another day, maybe two."

"Tell him you've been ralfing, he'll probably start panicking he got you pregnant."

Mary Sue lets out an annoyed laugh, and replies, "I don't give him enough sex-ed credit to be able to recognize those signs."

I send Duke a message, taking a page out of Mary Sue's book, letting him know I'm feeling under the weather so I'll have to take a rain check on seeing him again tonight. I get a message back a few minutes later, telling me to feel better. Fuck, he's a nice guy. It's really going to suck when I have to kill him.

I also send a message to Zeke, letting him know about my code theory—I don't know this for sure, but I presume it's likely there is a department of code breakers within the ranks of T.H.E.M. who would be better suited at finding and cracking a code than Mary Sue and I.

We arrive at the StopGame store where Bobby Anderson works—relieved to see Clark Jr.'s bicycle is *not* parked outside this time.

Walking into that game store, Mary Sue and I look like a couple of chickens who accidentally wandered into the reptile house at the San Francisco Zoo, and I realize too late we should have modified our wardrobe today, as Mary Sue and I—well, *Lindsay* and *Nanetta*—do not exactly look like your stereotypical female gamers. All it would've taken was a change of wardrobe and a slight hairstyle change, and we wouldn't raise a single eyebrow walking into a StopGame.

Don't give me that P.C. stereotyping crap. Look, I'm not saying this to be sexist or anything. Believe me, I know anyone can be a gamer, or a fisher, or a K-K-Fucking-K member, regardless of how they look or dress. That's not what I'm saying. Hell, I've been known to spend a weekend killing people on video games (ya know, when I'm not spending my weekend killing people in *real* life . . .)

However, I work in the field of deception. Making myself blend in and be inconspicuous requires being aware of how people view stereotypes and exploiting that to my advantage. So, if changing my wardrobe and hair to make me look more like a gamer than a legal assistant is what I have to do to avoid drawing attention to myself, then that is what I have to do.

As we walk through the store, I can feel Bobby's eyes following us—whether out of suspicion or randiness, I don't know and really don't want to know. Mary Sue and I share a glance, confirming we agree the sooner we get out of here, the better.

I grab the newest *Doom* game off the shelf—if nothing else, killing zombies and demonic hellions will make for a good stress reliever while I wait until we're ready to kill the Anderson Klan. While Clark Jr. rings up my purchase, Mary Sue discreetly places a bug under the lip of the counter.

As we walk out of the store, I feel Bobby's eyes following us out, and I'm glad—not for the first time—I ended up choosing Duke instead of his cousin.

We station ourselves again a way down the road, and spend the rest of the morning and early afternoon watching the store. Surprise, surprise: nothing happened. At three, the shift change arrives and we follow Bobby back to his home. Shortly after he disappears inside the house, we see Clark Jr. ride up on his bicycle, and go inside.

"Apparently the cousins are meeting up to play computer games," I remark.

"Wait . . . if Clark Jr. is here, and Becky's working the diner, and Clark Sr. is stalking Becky as usual, which means the Grobe house is probably empty," Mary Sue points out.

"You're probably right," I admit. "We don't know for sure if Timothy's there, but I doubt even Clark Jr. would be such a dolt as to leave his little brother home alone without any supervision."

I quickly link up my phone to the bug in the diner where Becky works, and confirm Becky and Clark Sr.

are indeed at the diner, meaning the Grobe house is most likely empty.

We turn the car around and drive to the Grobe house. We wait outside a few minutes, looking for any sign of Timothy being home alone, but no activity is detected.

We agree I will keep lookout from the car, while Mary Sue goes in and sets the bugs. Fortunately for us, a set of lock-picks is standard issue for all T.H.E.M. operatives. Fifteen minutes later, Mary Sue emerges from the house, and dashes back to the car.

Seeing as we have no idea when Clark Jr. or Timothy will be back, and we probably shouldn't linger in the area longer than necessary considering we just did a break-and-enter, we decide to call it a day and head back to Dickson, to start looking for clues in the murders that have been happening at the hotel.

While it may not have been the most enthralling day of surveillance I've ever done, it certainly was productive nonetheless. We not only bugged Bobby Anderson's place of work, but the actual Grobe house—that in itself was worth the hours of waiting tedium.

24

WE GET BACK to the hotel as twilight is settling in and return to my room to start breaking down Nick's latest string of killings. Seeing as I'm the one who discovered the code in Duluth, Mary Sue lets me take point on this exercise. We start off with my recapping how I stumbled upon Nick's code in the first place.

"I didn't just luck out and happen upon it right away," I begin. "I'd been going through the case files for several hours. I was starting to lose it, so I decided to go to square one and just list out each victim, like this."

It takes me a minute to recall every name, but one thing I've always been proud of is my memory. I wouldn't go as far as to say I have an eidetic memory, but pretty close to that. It's one of the reasons I hold grudges for so long.

Anyway, I eventually get it all written out, and then underline the first letter of each name on the list.

S̲usan Baker
A̲dam Jackson
R̲aven Arronson

<u>A</u>maranda Cosack
<u>H</u>enry Polls
<u>K</u>yle Andrews
<u>I</u>an Bond
<u>L</u>avanna Cox
<u>L</u>arry Wilkinson
<u>I</u>da Brown
<u>A</u>aron Belue
<u>N</u>athon Swanson

"Once I'd discovered that," I continue after showing Mary Sue the recreated list, "I reasoned this was his attempt at getting my attention, which meant there must have been more to the message than just my name."

"Makes sense," Mary Sue nods. "It's not like telling you your own name would be particularly useful to you."

"Exactly. So I started looking at other elements of each victim that might be a code—such as their ages. But I quickly realized whatever it was he'd coded would need to be an element he had control over. He had hand-picked each victim by their first name for the purpose of spelling out my name—that must have been tedious enough without singling them out by their ages, as well. That's when I remembered each victim had been taken and left at a location, *after* being murdered. So I listed out each location, in the same order they'd been killed, and came up with this:"

Again, I scribble out from memory a recreation of the list I'd made back in Duluth last fall, and underline the first letter of each location.

Chester Park
Orion Apartments
Marshall School
Enger Park
Erickson Road
Norwood Steet
Grant Park
Elinor Street
Russel Square
Tischer Creek
Web Woods
Riverside Park

"'Come Enger Twr,'" Mary Sue reads off the sheet of paper I hand to her. "Crafty son of a bitch."

"Exactly. Enger Tower is that tower in Enger park which overlooks the city. Once I'd decoded his message, I went to the tower and found him waiting for me."

"And yet remains the lingering question . . . *how* did he know when you'd gotten the message and were on your way to meet him?"

"Fucked if I know."

"You got plenty of that on Saturday, thank you very much."

I roll my eyes, but otherwise ignore her.

"So I think the best place for us to start is where I first found the code—listing out the names and seeing if anything stands out."

"Do you really think he'd do the same thing again?" Mary Sue asks, skeptically.

"No, probably not. He wouldn't want to make it easy. But it's a good place to start and that way we can at least rule it out."

"Fair enough," Mary Sue replies with a shrug. "So our first victim was the room service attendant, Craig."

"Hold on there," I interject, seeing an immediate problem. "Craig technically wasn't one of Nick's victims. *We* killed Craig, because he was one of Nick's henchman trying to kill us."

"Nanetta, think about it though," Mary Sue continues, standing her ground. "Do you *really* believe Nick thought 'Craig' was going to succeed at killing us? Even if he had been Nick's best assassin—which he clearly wasn't—the odds were two against one, especially considering you and I aren't exactly your everyday civilian assassination target."

"Why would he send one of his henchmen after us though, if he honestly believed we would beat him?"

"I can see a couple reasons," Mary Sue continues. "First and foremost, to get our attention and let us know he's already a step or two ahead of us, as usual—mission accomplished. Secondly, if 'Craig' was part of Nick's intended coded message, then it may have been worth it to him to 'sacrifice a pawn' for his ultimate endgame."

"Okay, I'm sold," I say, writing out Craig's name on a new piece of paper. "Besides, we can always take his name out later if it doesn't fit with anything else."

"Did we ever learn Craig's last name?" Mary Sue asks.

"No, but we can get that from Zeke. I'll make notes of any other gaps in our knowledge and send him an e-mail at the end of the night."

"Also—we should have him give us a list of any employees at the hotel who have just recently started. Help us narrow down our line of suspects."

"Good point," I say, as I scribble down another note on my list of questions for Zeke. "Okay, after Craig the Waiter, was Captain Weatherman."

"You mean Mr. Crowley," Mary Sue interjects with a smirk.

"Yeah, him. Did we get his first name?"

"Let me see, I got it somewhere . . . " Mary Sue fishes out her phone and starts fishing through her e-mails. After a few seconds, she perks up and says, "Walter."

"Walter Crowley, Captain Weatherman. It fits."

I add his name to the list.

Still consulting her e-mails, Mary Sue then adds, "The next two victims were Johnson Brown and Stephanie Webber."

Onto the list they go.

"Okay, so here is what we've got so far . . . " I say, handing my new list over to Mary Sue.

Craig ???
Walter Crowley
Johnson Brown
Stephanie Webber

"Just looking at that right now, I feel pretty confident in ruling out he's using the same code as last time," Mary Sue says, after glancing at the list. "Unless you can think of any words that start 'Cwjs'—even if we take Craig off the list, that doesn't help us any."

"No, it doesn't," I concede. "The last names don't really look promising, either—even without knowing Craig's last name, I'm pretty sure 'Cbw' doesn't spell anything."

We try a couple different tactics—last letter of each name, anagrams, etc.—before giving up on the name front.

"Oh well, it was worth a try," I admit in defeat.

"What next?"

"Let's try their ages—last time Nick picked the victims by their names, but maybe this time he *did* pick them by their age."

I add a new column to our list and write in the following:

Craig ???	???
Walter Crowley	48
Johnson Brown	33
Stephanie Webber	21

"Ignoring the fact we're missing information about Craig, this still isn't looking too promising," I reply. "The easiest code to do would be a numeric/alphabetic substitute—such as A = 1, B = 2, etc. However, there's only twenty-four letters in the alphabet, so 33 and 48 already rule that option out. It could still be a numeric/alphabetic substitute, just not something as obvious and easy as 1-2-3, A-B-C, but we'd need more of the complete code before we'd even have a chance at cracking *that*."

"Ooh, what about this!" Mary Sue exclaims as if she's found the map to El Dorado. "Look how the ages are descending—48, 33, 21. If we just take the first number in each age, that's 4-3-2."

"Yeah, but I'm pretty sure Craig wasn't in his fifties.

Also, I highly doubt Nick only has one more victim planned, so I'd guess that's just a coincidence."

"Oh," Mary Sue says, and it takes all my self control to keep from laughing at the look of disappointment on her face. "Alright, so we don't have enough information about their ages to really make any headway on that front just yet, what about their room numbers? That's something Nick could be using to pick them out."

"Absolutely, you're right," I retrieve my texts from Zeke with the data about each victim, and fill out another room number—placing *my* room as the location of Craig's death.

Craig ???	???	1236
Walter Crowley	48	1208
Johnson Brown	33	586
Stephanie Webber	21	669

"Let me guess . . . not enough information to work with yet?" Mary Sue sighs, rubbing the bridge of her nose as if warding off a headache.

"Yeah, I'm afraid not," I reluctantly concede. "I hate to say it, but we're gonna have to wait until Nick has killed a few more people before we even have a chance at figuring this out."

"Well, if we're lucky, Nick will continue on his current streak of killing one per day, so we should have enough to go on by the end of the week."

"Yeah, if *we're* lucky," I reply dryly.

Somehow, I seriously doubt we will turn out to be

so lucky. I'm pretty sure our allotment of good luck on this mission was used up today with our getting to bug the Grobe house so easily.

25

AFTER ALMOST AN entire week of sleeping through never-ending sex nightmares, I've more or less gotten used to waking up with every muscle in my body knotted and barely even register the tension coursing through every limb. I pull myself out of bed and cross to the window to look outside, fully expecting to see another caravan of Red and Blue cars clogging up the hotel parking lot. But, aside from the normal cars of the guests and staff of the hotel, the lot is empty. Not even one cop car in sight.

You'd think that would ease my concerns, but instead it heightens them. After consistently killing someone each night for the last three nights (four if you count Craig the Waiter—which I'm still not entirely convinced we should be), why would Nick—or whichever of his minions is currently stalking The Hotel Dickson—suddenly take a break? I try to tell myself maybe it's just the body hasn't been found yet, but I can't believe it would be that easy.

By this point, the spa receptionist has gone ahead and put me down preemptively on the schedule every morning, so I don't even have to call to make an appointment. As I walk through the lobby it appears confirmed there has not yet been any untoward activity discovered in the hotel. The staff seems tense, for sure, but after everything they'd undoubtedly been through over the last several days, that can hardly be taken as a surprise.

Once I'm done getting my morning feel-up—I mean, *massage* by Bill the Masseuse, I meet Mary Sue for breakfast and we discuss our plans for the day.

"As much as I'd like to," Mary Sue says, while shoveling buttermilk pancake into her mouth, "I don't think I can put off another date with Clark the Casanova. And you should probably see Duke again."

"Agreed," I say, hoping I don't sound too eager. I'm quickly losing hope that sleeping with Duke will help rid me of the nightmares, but I'm clinging to every last strand I can.

"Now that we've . . . *ahem* . . . *laid* the bait, we should start working on getting information out of them about what the family's up to."

"Yeah, absolutely."

No, I did not *completely* forget about that part of why I'm sleeping with Duke. Just *mostly* forgot . . . Shut up.

"Also, I suggest we give up trailing these dipshits, and just focus on bugging the rest of their houses. We've gotten nowhere by just following them, and I think our best chance of finding anything out is to bug them. We've got the Grobe house covered, so next we should do Don and Charlie's houses, then work on the apartments for Duke and John."

"If it means not spending another day in that damned car staring at empty country lanes, then I'm all for it," I attest.

Our plans settled, we each contact our respective suitors, making plans to meet up later that night, and then head out. Still, no sign of any police activity anywhere in the hotel. Once we are in the isolation of the car, I share my concern with Mary Sue.

"I'm sure it's nothing, they probably just haven't found the body yet," she replies with a shrug. "Guarantee you, by the time we get back tonight the place will be crawling with fuzz again."

I can't tell if she is just saying this to make me feel better, or if her seemingly endless supply positivity really is making her believe what she says. It's often hard to tell with Mary Sue.

We get out to Bucksnort and find our way to Don Anderson's home. It doesn't take long to determine the house is vacant—no cars, no sign of activity, etc. Once we're sure it's safe, we trade places from yesterday and Mary Sue sits watch in the car while I go in to place the bugs.

I don't really know what I had been expecting the house to look like on the inside, but I admit it is a letdown. I guess it would have been absurd to really expect to bc greeted by candelabra marked with swastikas, and sets of white hooded robes hanging in the closet, but still. The house is boringly plain and yields little evidence that its inhabitants are a bunch of white supremacist neo-Nazis. A crucifix over the fireplace. Family pictures hanging from the walls. Closets filled with every day leisure clothes and a few 'Sunday Best' outfits. Hell, I even lift up the rug in the living room to see if there's a hidden trapdoor leading to Don's Nefarious Klan Cave Lair, but nothing. Just plain, boring, floorboards. Blah.

I place a bug in each room of the house, and then make my hasty departure before anyone should happen to return home.

Next we find Charlie Anderson's house—unfortunately, we aren't as lucky as we were with Duke's house, as we find Charlie's wife, Linda, home tending to her garden at the back of the house. We park a few houses down and wait for Linda to head out for groceries or some errand that will free up the house for us.

We are on the verge of giving up and trying this house on another day, when Linda *finally* pulls out of the house in a beat-up Ford Escape. Mary Sue takes point again, while I stand watch from the car.

By the time she returns, we assess how much time we have left before we need to head back to Dickson to get ready for our dates tonight, and decide we have time to plant one more set of bugs, in either Duke's or John's apartment. I suggest we do Duke's, as I know he's at work.

At first I'm not sure how I feel about bugging the apartment of a guy I'm sleeping with, but then I think about the fact I murdered many of the guys I slept with, and suddenly spying doesn't seem like that grave of an offense.

Being an apartment instead of an individual house, it's a bit harder to be completely sure no one's home—but unless Duke left work early or has a roommate we weren't able to find any information about, it should be safe.

It's my turn to take point this time around, and I admit it does feel a little awkward to be discovering this aspect of Duke's life without him. His apartment is about what you'd expect for a twenty-something bachelor pad. Empty pizza boxes strewn about (at least they're empty and not moldy—I have to give him credit for *that* at least), dirty shirts and underwear spread haphazardly across the floor, a path leading through the various piles of debris to the kitchen, bedroom, bathroom, and living room. But honestly, I've seen worse as far as bachelor pads go.

I don't spend much time in the living room and kitchen, just long enough to plant the necessary bugs and move on. But when I get to the bedroom . . . I can't explain what changed, but being in that most sacred of rooms of the man whom I most recently slept with, it feels . . . well, *wrong*—but *exhilarating* in that wrongness. Obviously, I'm not exactly the most moral of people, so I shouldn't be surprised that violating Duke's most private sanctum would appeal to me.

I take my time exploring his bedroom, every nerve in my body tingling with each taboo explored. Even though there's nothing particularly revealing about the room—the clothes in his dresser are more or less the same style he has worn on his dates with me—it still feels like I'm discovering new sides of him.

Feeling particularly impish, I lift up his mattress— I'm not in the least surprised to find a couple nudey mags waiting to be found. What I was *not* expecting, however, was a printed-out copy of my—well, *Nanetta's,* Facespace profile picture. On some level, I know I should be grossed out—I hold no delusions as to what purpose he printed the photo out for—but I'm actually kinda flattered.

Look, I'm not saying I have a low opinion of my looks or anything, but I just never really thought of myself as the kind of girl a guy would necessary do *that* to. True, it's 'Nanetta' and not the 'real' me he's looking at, but I've been doing this undercover bullshit for so many years, long ago I gave up the pretense of differentiating between how people react to my Dupe appearance and how people react to my real appearance.

Suddenly, after having made this discovery, the intrusion of Duke's space feels wrong again. I quickly replace the mags and profile photo, and place a bug underneath the lamp on his bed, then make a hasty departure.

"Took you long enough," Mary Sue quips as I climb back into the Skank Mobile. "What, were you sniffing his boxers or something?"

"Don't be a pervert," I retort. I try to place as much disgust into the sentence as I possibly can, but I'm afraid even I—master sociopathic spy—can't hide the awkwardness I feel after my discoveries in Duke's bedroom.

My transparency must be even worse than I feared, because Mary Sue just replies with a "Hmmm" and pulls out onto the road without another word. To cover up the awkward silence, she puts on the original cast album of *Wicked*—let me tell you, if I *never* hear Mary Sue sing *Popular* again in my life, it will have been too soon.

When we get back to the hotel, I text Zeke to find out if there was another body found today, and he confirms my suspicions that there were no murders at the hotel last night.

Later that evening, after Mary Sue has already left to meet up with Clark Jr., I get a text from Duke that he's on his way. By this point, the awkward feeling of having found my picture under his bed has turned into full-on yearning, and so I reply to his text, telling him to just come straight to my room. As extra motivation, I take a selfie of myself in my slinkiest negligee and send it to him. He makes the usually thirty minute drive in just under twenty minutes. Damn, I'm good.

We're both so hungry with need we skip the foreplay this time—which is fine with me. Unfortunately, the desire to kill him does rear its ugly head—it seems Jason truly is the only man I can sleep with more than once without wanting to kill him. But I force myself not to give into the temptation, and I'm surprised to find that withholding my murderous urges actually makes the actual sex *so* much more intense. It's probably a good thing I didn't discover this sooner . . .

We keep at it until almost midnight, with a few breaks here and there to catch our breath, when Duke tiredly admits he needs to go if he's going to make it to work in the morning. For a moment, I'm tempted to ask him to stay the night and leave for work in the morning, but considering the darker turn my dreams have taken and my most recent urge to slit his throat mid-coitus, I decide it probably would not be a good idea to entrust Duke in the care of my subconscious self.

I kiss him goodnight at the door, and return to my bed, cursing Nanetta for being foolish enough as to let me fall so dangerously for someone. It makes me actually relieved I am going to have to kill him in the near future—at least I won't have to worry about being in love with him anymore after that . . .

26

BY THIS POINT, you should be able to see where this is going. Once again, last night's activities did nothing to free me of my cursed nocturnal visions. On the plus side, the dreams did not get more horrific this time, like they did after Saturday night. It's a small blessing, but I'll take it.

On the bright side, when I look out the window I see the parking it is once again lit up by cop cars, so it seems Nick is back on schedule. Yay, for that . . .

I send Zeke a text, asking for more information about the newest kill and then head down to the spa for my daily spa appointment. Apparently Bill's gotten more comfortable with me over the last week, 'cause he goes a bit further south on my backrub than he has so far. I don't raise any objections, though, because there's plenty of tension in that area, too. I briefly consider suddenly flipping over and seeing just how willing Bill is to risk losing his job (seeing as Duke isn't doing the trick to get rid of my fucking sex-mares, maybe Bill will get the job done), but decide that would only complicate everything.

After my massage, I meet Mary Sue at the hotel restaurant for breakfast again.

"So, did you get any intel last night from Duke?" she asks as soon as our waitress has left to get our drinks.

"Oh . . . no . . . I tried, but . . . uh . . . he wasn't very forthcoming . . . "

Okay, yeah. I kinda forgot about that part of the plan completely, this time . . . Oops. Mary Sue unfortunately is not fooled by my brilliant improvisations.

"For fuck's sake, Nanetta," she snaps. "I'm out there working my ass off, and you're just sitting back having the time of your life with your little boy toy."

"It's not like that," I hiss, hoping nobody else in the restaurant overheard her outburst. "I told you my reasons for dating Duke have more to do with than just the mission. Hell, I didn't even *want* to get into this at all in the beginning, remember?"

"Yeah, I remember," Mary Sue replies, still clearly irritated.

"The only reason I started seeing him at all was because I wanted to make these fucking nightmares I'm having stop. That, unfortunately, is not working. I could stop seeing him until the mission is over–"

"No, if you do that he might get suspicious, and that could jeopardize the mission," Mary Sue interjects, and I see her anger weakening.

"Exactly. So, since my original intent clearly isn't working to plan, I will keep seeing him until we're done, but I will now be able to focus on trying to get information out of him, instead of getting rid of these damn dreams."

"Okay, okay. You're right. I'm sorry I snapped. I'm just irritated, 'cause I'm off boinking Clark Jr. the

Louse and not getting anything—sexual or informational."

"Still can't find the clit, huh?"

"I swear, if that asshole tries to lick my belly button one more fucking time, I'm going to fucking rip his head off with my thighs. And he's not budging on information, either. I tried to get him to tell me what his plans are for the weekend, but he just lied and said he's playing poker. If I could just get *something* useful out of this dipshit—either a decent orgasm or some information—I'd at least feel like my efforts were worthwhile, but I'm getting *nothing*."

"I'm sorry. I promise, I've given up any hope on these dreams going away now, so going forward I will focus on getting information out of him."

My transgression forgiven, we finish our breakfast and head out to the Skank Mobile. As we leave, I get a text from Zeke, responding to my earlier inquiry about the latest victim. Today's lucky winner is Jessica Baker, a 24 year-old female, killed in room 587. A scream was reported by a guest in her neighboring room—585—around 3 am, by the time the night manager arrived to investigate the disturbance, Jessica was already slit open and her killer had vanished.

"Okay, the fact he didn't kill anybody yesterday has to mean something, right?" Mary Sue asks, as we pull out of the hotel parking lot.

"Yeah, but what?"

"If there *is* a code, then it's most likely representing a break in the message."

"Like a new word, or how his first code had two parts; first my name to catch my attention, and then the instructions of where to meet him."

"Yeah, something like that."

"If it *does* represent a new word in his message, then each kill probably represents one letter—so the first word in his message is only three or four letters. That's a good start, at least."

As we drive out to Bucksnort, I pull up the audio feed of the bug we placed in the CD store where John Anderson works, to verify he is working that morning, and luckily for us he is. We know from our research John does have a roommate, a buddy from college, so that may complicate things if he happens to be home, so we'll have to be a tad more careful.

Fortunately, when we get to John's apartment building, we find his apartment is on the ground floor, so it proves fairly easy to do a little snooping and verify that John's roommate is not home, either.

Mary Sue takes point this time, while I stand watch, and fifteen short minutes later we're headed back to Dickson, having completed our bugging of each of the Anderson Klan's homes.

As Mary Sue drives, I text Duke asking if he can come over again tonight (Mary Sue already fed Clark Jr. an excuse she had to work late tonight, but as I need to start work on getting information from Duke, I can't afford to waste any more time), and he replies he'll be over right after he gets off work.

We get back to the Hotel Dickson and as we step off the elevator on the twelfth floor, we run into Tim the Bellman, apparently having just completed assisting a check-in. He looks particularly pale—even for his usual pasty self.

"Is everything alright, Tim?" Mary Sue asks.

"Well . . . I'm not supposed to talk about it, but I

guess there's no point in pretending you ladies haven't noticed everything that's . . . happened over the last week, here."

"We'd have to be blind idiots not to notice," I respond.

Tim nods sadly, then continues, "There's been a lot of talk around the staff—if they can't find whoever's . . . doing all of this, they're going to have to close the hotel down again, probably for good this time."

"Surely the police must have some leads," Mary Sue says comfortingly, though we both know a pro like Nick Jin sure as hell ain't gonna make things easy for anyone.

"I don't know," Tim replies darkly. "I overheard two of the managers saying nothing is showing up on any of the surveillance footage, and even the key readers—machines that should record every time a hotel room door is opened—aren't giving them any information. They're starting to think . . . I think they're starting to think it's someone on the staff."

Mary Sue and I share a meaningful look, as we had already suspected as much ourselves.

"I'm sorry, I gotta get back down to the bell desk. You ladies have yourselves a good afternoon, okay?"

"Of course, Tim," Mary Sue says, giving him a comforting pat on the shoulder. "Don't worry, I'm sure they'll find this creep soon enough and everything will get back to normal here."

I wish I could believe Mary Sue's words of comfort, but I'm pretty sure even if the police managed to catch Nick, the hotel's reputation for being the location of multiple grisly murders will be a stain not easy to recover from.

We go back to my room and start listening through the surveillance audio we've gotten from the bugs so far. We don't really learn anything particularly pertinent to the case, however we do discover Clark Sr. is beating Becky—a revelation that is not exactly startling to either Mary Sue or myself, and only furthers our desire to get on with this mission and kill the fucking bastard. Hell, if Mary Sue weren't with me right now on this assignment, I'd probably lose my cool and drive out to Bucksnort to spill open the fat pig's lardy gut.

But, as often happens, Mary Sue helps me keep my cool, just by simply being there and forcing me to have to think about someone other than myself. Although I can tell from her flaring nostrils she is just as enraged as I am, and I suspect it's probably requiring a great deal of her own self control to refrain from driving out to Bucksnort, also.

A year ago, I would have completely reeled at the idea of having to work with someone else on an assignment (in fact, I *did* reel when Zeke first informed me I would be working with Mary Sue in Duluth), but now I can't imagine going on an assignment without her. I both hate and secretly like the change she has made in me.

27

WE STOP OUR investigations late in the afternoon when I get a call from Duke letting me know he's on his way. Knowing that I need to work on getting information out of him, I suggest we meet at the coffee shop on the corner and he agrees (though I'm sure he wouldn't protest if I asked him to come straight to my room again . . .)

Half an hour later, I'm sitting at our usual table in the coffee shop, and my fucking traitorous heart skips a couple beats when Duke walks in the door.

We hug, kiss each other on the cheek, and order our coffees. Duke talks about a beat-up old Chevy he's working on at the shop which is probably on its last legs. I make up a story about how the 'lawyer I'm working for' is a total ass who is constantly trying to get in my pants. Basic small talk—stuff I usually hate engaging in, but for some reason I don't mind it so much with Duke (partly because I don't actually have to be honest with him about my side of things).

"So, do you have any plans for the weekend?" I ask, putting a coy lilt to the words to give him the impression that I'm hoping he'll have time to spend with me.

"Not much. Just a poker game with my fam'ly and some friends on Saturday night," he says with a shrug.

He's good. For the most part, I'm pretty good at knowing when someone is lying to me. But if it weren't for the fact that I know otherwise, I wouldn't suspect a thing from his claim. Clearly the whole Klan has agreed to use a poker game as the excuse for their meetings, seeing as that's what Clark Jr. told Mary Sue, also.

"Nothing else planned?" I ask again, hoping I don't rouse his suspicions.

"Nope, that's all I've got for the weekend. My Pa'll be manning the shop this weekend, so I'm off."

"Well, maybe we can go to a movie or something Saturday afternoon before your game, then."

"That would be nice," he replies with a sincere smile.

I know if I push the questioning any further, I will only rouse his suspicion so I drop the matter and we finish our drinks over more idle chat.

"So . . . shall we . . . ?" he awkwardly asks, as he finishes of the last sip of his coffee.

Internally, I secretly want to decline his offer. The sex is clearly not doing the trick I hoped it would, as far as making might nightmares stop, so really the only function this relationship is currently serving is for work-related intelligence gathering.

However, I don't want him to grow suspicious or think I'm losing interest—and thereby damage my chances of actually getting any useful information out of him, and so I show no external sign of my internal dilemma and respond with an arched eyebrow and a smile.

The urge to murder him mid-coitus is even worse this time—which is odd, because I really *do* like the guy. But damn it, that doesn't stop me front wanting to plunge a nice, cold, sharp blade into his soft, moist gut and slide it around until he never moves again.

Yes. I know I have issues. This is not news to anyone.

The payoff I discovered last night—that holding in my baser murderous desires leads to an even more intense climax—still holds true, but this time it's not enough to leave me actually satisfied. Satisfied, maybe, but not *satisfied*.

Either I'm a better actor than I realize, or Duke is just another clueless douche-bag male, because he doesn't seem to pick up on my disappointed afterglow. To give him and myself each a little credit, it's probably a bit of both.

Saturday is almost three days away now, and I seriously can't wait. Come Saturday night, we will finally be able to overhear the Anderson Klan's 'poker game,' so we'll know for sure what it is they are planning and be able to plan our attack against them accordingly before they pull it off.

I have a hard time reminding myself that the man lying next to me, still panting in post-orgasmic glow, is in fact a hate-filled, White Supremacist Klan member. The Duke I have been dating and the Duke I know him to be for real seem like two completely different people, and I just can't bring myself to reconcile them.

But then I remind myself Duke himself just finished banging a woman he believes to be a hardworking legal assistant, but is in fact a heartless, sociopathic, professional serial killer.

My bed, tonight, is clearly encumbered with an abundance of doppelgängers . . .

28

THE NEXT TWO DAYS, pass in pretty much the same fashion. I wake up tense after a night of incessant nightmares and find the parking lot of the hotel plagued with flashing red and blue lights (Thursday morning's victim was Kirk Arce, a 45 year-old male killed in room 329, and Friday's was Sandra Campbell, a 36 year-old female killed in room 710). I get my daily massage from Bill the Masseuse. Mary Sue and I spend the day listening to surveillance tapes. In the evenings, Mary Sue visits Clark Jr. (who still can't find the 'magic button') and unsuccessfully tries to get information out of him, while I meet up with Duke and have equal success getting information out of him, followed by admittedly great sex which still leaves me wanting to slice him open with a knife. Duke leaves, Mary Sue gets back to the hotel and we compare useless notes, I go to bed and the nonsense starts all over again.

Saturday morning starts much the same, except I wake up knowing this madness is almost over. Well, at least the madness of my mission to kill the Anderson Klan. Who knows how much longer I'm gonna have to deal with the unending nightmares and the hunt for Nick Jin. That's a different question altogether.

Of course, there's another murder, and Zeke texts me the information as always (by this point, he's already started checking each morning without even bothering to wait for my asking him for information). Maria Avila, a 54 year-old female found in room 480.

I meet Duke in the afternoon for our movie date. I really hadn't wanted to go to a RomCom, 'cause I normally hate those damn things. However, I'm pretty sure my tendency to laugh my ass off throughout horror movies—my preferred genre of theatrical entertainment—would be a break of character for Nanetta and would risk breaking my cover, so instead I suggest the latest chick-flick-snore-fest, and do my best to play the part of a love-sick damsel instead of barfing my guts out.

After the movie, Duke has to leave in order to make it to his 'poker game.' He drops me off at the hotel and I meet Mary Sue back at my room where we tap into the feed for the Bucksnort Town Hall so we can finally find out what the Anderson Klan is planning and make our own plans accordingly.

As we wait, half-listening to the feed for the arrival of the Anderson Klan, Mary Sue brings up Nick Jin's latest yet-to-be-cracked code.

"I've been thinking more and more about that day without a murder," she says, her brows knit in thought, "and the more I think about it, the more it seems it has to be a planned break in the code."

"I agree, but that doesn't help us figure out where it is Nick's telling us to go . . . " I say, and then suddenly that glow-stick-filled severed scrotum light pops up over my head again.

"Fuck me 'til Sunday . . . " I say, unable to believe I didn't think of this sooner.

"While I certainly could use it, I think you've been taken care of in *that* department this last week, sweetie," Mary Sue smirks.

"Shut up, I think I figured it out. He *is* telling us where he wants us to meet him. If I'm right, he's telling us *exactly* where to meet him."

"What are you rambling about?" Mary Sue asks.

"Just gimme a sec," I say, pulling out our notepad of our previous attempts to break Nick's code.

I contemplate for a second on where to start with my idea, and decide the victims' ages would be easiest, and sketch out another graph at the bottom of the page.

Craig Nelson	22
Walter Crowley	48
Johnson Brown	33
Stephanie Webber	21
Jessica Baker	24
Kirk Arce	45
Sandra Campbell	36
Maria Avila	54

Finished with my sketching, I turn the notepad so Mary Sue can see what I've written down, and say, "What if Nick isn't just sending us a coded message—what if he's sending us *precise coordinates* of where he wants us to meet him?"

"You mean like GPS coordinates?" Mary Sue asks, and I can see the glowing scrotum sack light up over her head as well.

"Exactly," I reply, glad she caught on quickly. "A GPS coordinate would be two sets of eight digits—"

"And the day without any murders would represent the break between the two numbers," Mary Sue adds, filling in my next thought for me.

"Yes. I started here with the victims' ages, since they were all two digit numbers, and would be easiest to convert into a GPS coordinate."

"So next we hit the internet and see where it brings us?" Mary Sue asks.

"Exactly."

I pull out my phone's GPS navigator app, and type in: 22.483321, -24.453654—which brings up a point that is about 500 miles off the coast of Africa in the Northern Atlantic Ocean.

"I'm thinking that's not right," Mary Sue says.

"No, definitely not," I concede. "I thought the ages would probably be too much of a stretch for Nick to have selected his victims based on, but it made a decent starting place."

"What else is there to try, though, that would be practical for him to have selected each victim?"

"Well, there's the room number of each victim, but there are too many digits for it to be a GPS coordinate, if that's the case. Each room is either three or four digits long . . . "

"What if we just use the last two digits of each room number?" Mary Sue suggests.

"So 1236 would just be 36?" I ask, considering the possibility.

"Yes, exactly."

"It's worth a shot," I concede and start copying down another chart of the victims and their room numbers.

Craig Nelson	36
Walter Crowley	08
Johnson Brown	86
Stephanie Webber	69
Jessica Baker	87
Kirk Arce	29
Sandra Campbell	10
Maria Avila	80

"Hold onto your butts," I say, as I type the following sequence into the GPS app on my phone: 36.088669, -87.291080

This time, the results pull up a spot in the middle of Montgomery State Park—a park about seven miles outside of Dickson.

"I'd call that a jackpot," Mary Sue says.

"Jack-fucking-pot, indeed," I concur.

29

WE AGREE TO put off our surveillance of the Anderson Klan's town hall meeting— everything will be recorded and available for us to listen to when we come back. Settling things with Nick Jin is a far higher priority. And of course we don't leave un-armed, we each sport a handgun, and I also have my favorite knife in a scabbard tucked under the waistband of my jeans.

After a fifteen minute drive to Montgomery Bell State Park, we find a campground to park the Skank Mobile, and make the remaining trek on foot, following the directions on my phone to a quaint old log cabin-style church. A plaque outside reads 'First Cumberland Presbyterian Church.'

"This must be it," Mary Sue whispers. "This reeks of an ambush . . . "

"I know, but it was just Nick that met me at Enger Tower in Duluth, so maybe it'll just be him again . . . " I whisper back, not really sure how much I believe the words myself.

"Well, either way, we might as well do what we came here to do," Mary Sue whispers, and I'm glad this time I at least have her with me.

After an easy pick of the church door's lock, we cross the threshold into Cumberland Church. The church is small, but the darkness within is immense. The door creaks shut behind us, sacrilegiously tarnishing the silence.

As soon as the reverberations of the door's slam have faded into the echoes of the darkness, a familiar voice speaks out.

"Hello Sara, I'm glad you brought Mary Sue with you this time."

Out of the shadows into a sliver of moonlight coming through one of the chapel windows, steps an old man, who looks slightly familiar. After a few moments of confusion, I realize where I recognize him from—Mr. Jorra, the old man who checked into the Hotel Dickson ahead of Mary Sue and myself the night we first arrived.

"I would've come with her last time, but there was that whole thing where I was in critical care, thanks to you trying to kill me," Mary Sue replies, venom seeping from every word.

"Misk, please," Nick says, reverting to Mary Sue's T.H.E.M. code name. "If I'd wanted you dead in Duluth, I would've had it done. I needed Sarah alone then, though, which is why I . . . put you temporarily out of service."

"Enough of all this bull shit," I snap impatiently. "Let's get to the point. What do you want with us, Nick?"

"Always the direct approach, Sarah," Nick smiles fondly. "I appreciate that. I invited you both here tonight because I hoped maybe, with Misk's help, I might be able to convince both of you to join our cause against T.H.E.M."

"Why would I help convince Sarah to join you?" Mary Sue snaps.

"Sarah, as you know, can be a little hot-headed," Nick replies. "No doubt her anger over my manipulation of her in Duluth influenced her judgment about the offer I made to her. I hope if I make my case to the both of you together, you will see I'm right and be able to agree between each of you that you should join us."

"And if we don't join you?" I ask.

Nick shrugs noncommittally and says, "I have explicit instructions from my partner not to kill you, Sarah, but that doesn't mean I can't make your life *very* miserable. You think those dreams I've been planting in your mind this last week have been torturous? You haven't seen *anything*, yet."

A shiver runs down my spine. Of course, at the back of my mind I'd suspected all along that Nick was somehow responsible for my nightly subconscious haunting, but the idea was so impossible I never really allowed myself to seriously consider the possibility. But even though I have no reason to believe Nick, as soon as he says the words I know they are true. And as bad as the last week has been, I do not doubt Nick's threat that death would be preferable to whatever mental torture he could force upon me.

"What do you think you could possibly have to say that you didn't say to me in Duluth?" I retort, trying to keep any quaver out of my voice.

"I realized in hindsight I should have been more forthcoming with you in Duluth," Nick confesses. "In subsequent meetings with T.H.E.M. operatives, as you know I was more successful at gaining supporters, because I better explained my motivations and reasoning for turning against T.H.E.M. But to be fair to myself, you weren't exactly over-anxious to hear me out, were you Sarah? I hope that Misk's more tolerant nature will convince you, this time, to hear me out before trying to fight me again."

I look to Mary Sue, and see that she is as skeptical as I am, but she shrugs and says, "We came here for answers, didn't we? Only way we'll get them is to hear what he has to say. Then we can kill the smug bastard."

Nick smirks, "You can try at least."

We both shoot him glares of daggers, but he ignores us and begins. "As you know, I was disbanded from T.H.E.M. when I had a 'mental breakdown' several years ago and was thereafter committed. What you don't know is that my breakdown was, in fact, a direct result of T.H.E.M.'s influence.

"For many years, T.H.E.M. has been wanting to explore the technology of mind control. Zeke's idea was he could *temporarily* program someone— anyone—to become an agent for a specific amount of time, and then release them. The subject would continue on with their life, unaware they had been used as a pawn in a contract murder. I'm sure you can see why this would appeal to Zeke. Why risk a valued T.H.E.M. agent on a dangerous assignment if he can program a random civilian to do the job instead? If the civilian got caught or killed, at least Zeke wouldn't have lost a valued agent in the process."

Back when Nick had first told me T.H.E.M. was up to more than I knew about, I scoffed at the idea. After all, I'm obviously aware that they pay serial killers to do what they do best, so what could possibly be worse than that? However, as someone who takes her free will and independence *very* seriously, the idea of T.H.E.M. being able to control me against my will . . . that definitely crosses a line I'm not exactly thrilled about. True, according to Nick's scenario, they would be utilizing the mind control on civilians, and not T.H.E.M. operatives such as myself, but what would *really* stop them from using it against their operatives, as well? Zeke's word? I trust Zeke's word about as far as I could throw the fat bastard—which is to say not very.

"About five years ago," Nick continues, his expression unreadable, "they developed a serum which would assist with their mind control efforts, and sought out a few select volunteers to experiment on. I was one of those volunteers. Had I known what would happen . . . well, that is neither here nor there. In a nutshell, T.H.E.M.'s mind control serum worked—but it worked a little *too* well. Certainly better than they had anticipated.

"There were certain . . . ah, *side effects* which came along with the serum. In addition to turning the brain into a temporary puppet, it *opened up* the brain's potential, even after the mind control was released."

"So, what, they turned you into a super brain?" I ask, trying not to roll my eyes as I do so.

"No, they didn't increase my intelligence, really," Nick responds, apparently oblivious to my sarcasm. "More like they expanded the dormant potential of what my brain was already capable of. When I woke up from 'the sleep'—the term they used for the period when I would be under their control—I found I could hear the thoughts of those around me."

"A psychic. Really? You seriously expect us to believe this horseshit?" Mary Sue snorts.

I want to side with Mary Sue's skepticism, but I must confess this explains a lot of questions that have been daunting me the last several months.

"That's how you were able to know things about me I never told *anyone;* how you knew when I was going to Enger Tower, and tonight that we were coming here to the church; how you've stayed one step ahead of T.H.E.M. at so many turns."

"Yes, exactly," Nick nods.

I chance a sideways glance at Mary Sue, and see her skepticism begin to crack, if not completely crumble.

"My 'mental breakdown,'" Nick continues, "was in fact an episode induced while I was in the sleep. T.H.E.M. realized having an agent who could read their minds was not in their best interest, so they put me into the sleep and forced me to have that public mental breakdown as an excuse to disavow my services and have me locked up. When I emerged from the sleep, I found myself in a padded cell with no recollection of how I got there.

"If you're under the influence of their mind control," Mary Sue interjects, "why haven't they just 'put you into the sleep' since you broke out?"

"It doesn't work that way," Nick replies, curtly. "They have to inject me with the serum in order to control me, though the *other side effects* remain."

"And the dreams you've been giving me?" I ask, not bothering to hide the anger in my voice over that particular violation—a violation even worse than when he tricked me into sleeping with him in Duluth. "I suppose that's another *side effect?*"

"Yes," Nick replies, unfazed by the scorn in my voice. "It was not one of the first side effects I experienced, but during my years in prison I discovered that particular talent and was able to experiment on the other inmates until I perfected it."

"And you've been using the serum as well, haven't you?" Mary Sue asks. "On Senator Keeley back in L.A., and Craig the Waiter at the hotel."

"Very astute of you," Nick nods. "While I was imprisoned, T.H.E.M. perfected the serum and was able to get rid of the 'little bug' which empowered the subjects with mind-sight, as I call it. Through the agents I was able to convince to come over to my side, I have gotten a copy of the formula and have used it, when necessary."

"So you're no better than T.H.E.M., if you're using the same formula that made you turn against them," Mary Sue points out.

"T.H.E.M. abandoned me!" Nick screams—revealing, as he did once or twice back in Enger Tower, the madness lying under his otherwise cool façade. He calms himself and continues, "T.H.E.M. needs to be stopped—by any means necessary. Once I have successfully brought T.H.E.M. down and revealed them for what they are, I will destroy the formula and all remaining vials."

"How noble of you," I quip.

"Enough," Nick snaps. "I've told you everything I have to tell. Are you with us, or against us?"

"You clearly haven't told us everything there is to tell," Mary Sue points out. "What about this 'partner' of yours? Who are they, and why aren't they here, making their own case?"

Nick's face darkens. "The identity of my partner is not my secret to disclose. Suffice to say, this is the final offer we are willing to extend to the both of you to join our cause. If you will not join us, then you stand with T.H.E.M. and your choice will seal your fates."

I look to Mary Sue, and I can see we are in agreement. As unsettled as I am at the idea of T.H.E.M. tampering with my free will, it's not enough to make me turn rogue and bite the hand which has kept me safe and fed for most of my adult life. If it weren't for T.H.E.M., I would have been put into a gas chamber years ago, if I was lucky, or worse, spending the rest of my days rotting away in a jail cell, like my mother.

Besides, as unsettled as I am at the idea of T.H.E.M. controlling me against my will, I'm far more unsettled by Nick Jin and his abuse and manipulations of my psyche, so joining forces with *him* is definitely not an option.

"No, Nick," I respond turning back to face our opponent. "We're not with you."

"So be it," Nick replies simply.

I barely register the subtle flick of his wrist, or the swoosh of the air, but I definitely register the wet *thwop* to my left.

I look over, and I see a knife emerging from Mary Sue's neck, blood already freely flowing from the wound.

30

"**WHAT THE FUCK?**" I scream, rushing to Mary Sue's side, even though I already know there is nothing I can do to help her. "You said–"

"I said I had explicit instructions not to kill *you*, Sarah," Nick replies with a bored shrug, as if we were discussing something as mundane as the weather, not his murdering my only friend in the world. "I didn't say anything about Mary Sue."

I raise my handgun to shoot, but Nick has already disappeared into the shadows. I spin around, searching every shadow for some sign of my foe.

Suddenly, I feel Nick's foot sharply connect with my back and I am pushed forward, my handgun clattering across the floor of the church as the wind is knocked out of me.

As I try to regain my breath, Nick flips me onto my back and sits on my stomach, straddling my torso between his thighs, and further pushing what wind was left out of my struggling lungs.

"I said it in Duluth, Sara, and I'll say it again," Nick breathes menacingly into my ear. "It's too bad you aren't willing to take me up on my offer. We could have had such *fun* together."

Lucky for me Nick, as usual, is too busy thinking with his penis to notice my hand slipping to the knife hidden in my waistband. With what strength I have left, I take the knife and lunge it into his side.

As Nick screams in agony and topples off of me, my breath finally returns to me and I gasp in the sweet, sweet, oxygen which I'd been taking for granted until the last few moments.

"You fucking cunt," Nick screams, as he regains his footing and aims a kick at my head.

Either my training with Mary Sue paid off or Nick's slowed down enough by the injury I inflicted, but either way I manage to dodge his kick and use the opportunity of his exposure to lodge a solid punch into his groin.

As Nick collapses to the floor, I scramble away, vainly searching through the darkness for my lost handgun. I hear Nick recovering, and barely manage to duck into a shadow before he has risen.

"You're really making it difficult for me oblige my partner's request, Sarah," Nick rasps into the silence of the church. "They will be disappointed, no doubt, if you end up like your friend Misk, but they will understand if you leave me with no choice."

I stay as still as possible as Nick hunts through the shadows for me. A tiny glint of moonlight reflects in the darkness, and I see the handgun on the floor, between me and Nick. Unfortunately, it's closer to him than it is to me, and if I went for it he'd surely get there first.

But either way, it's only a matter of time before he finds me, so I decide to take the gamble and go for it anyway.

Nick sees me running, and in a split second sees what I'm running for, and cuts me off to my quarry with a solid roundhouse kick into the side of my ribcage. We both scream in unison, me as Nick's kick lands home, and Nick as the move strains the wound I left in his side.

I collapse in a painful heap onto Mary Sue's lifeless body, as Nick—panting from pain—claims the handgun I had vainly tried to reclaim. I feel something hard digging into my back, and it takes me a moment to realize it's the gun Mary Sue had been carrying—I'd gotten so caught up in reclaiming my gun, I'd forgotten she had one as well.

"Fuck it," Nick rasps, aiming my handgun at me from several feet away. "My partner will just have to–"

I never find out what Nick's partner will have to do, because as fast as I can, I pull the handgun from Mary Sue's lifeless grip and fire off a shot. A black dot appears in the middle of Nick's forehead as he flies backward and collapses in a lifeless heap of spasming limbs on the church floor.

I limp back to where Mary Sue and I had parked the Skank Mobile, and then drive it to the church, ramming down the road barricade set up by the park rangers when they closed the park for the night. If Zeke wants to bill me for the damages to the car, he can go ahead.

I probably should just let the extraction team take care of both Mary Sue and Nick's bodies, but I can't stand to think of Mary Sue being unceremoniously chopped up and sucked into vacuum bags. She deserves better than that. What I'm exactly going to do with her, I haven't figured out just yet—it's not like I'll exactly be able to shove her in my suitcase and take her back to L.A. All I know is I can't let her fall prey to the Yuppy Aryans.

It takes all of my waning strength to haul Mary Sue's lifeless body out of the church and into the trunk of the Skank Mobile, but I get it done.

As I drive back to the Hotel Dickson, I call Zeke and tell him about what happened. I'm still numb, and I barely register his response. I'm sure whatever he says is probably supposed to sound heartfelt and sincere, but I really don't give a fuck right now.

I tell him an extraction team will need to come in ASAP and clean up the church, get rid of Nick's body, and repair the gate I ran down. I tell him I'll be taking care of Mary Sue's body. For once, Zeke is smart enough not to ask me any questions. In return, I do not ask him any questions about the information Nick gave me. I don't have the energy for those answers right now. But soon, Zeke, *very* soon you *will* be answering.

Zeke tells me to finish up the Anderson Klan assignment, and get back to L.A. at the first opportunity, and needless to say I've never been so eager to follow an order.

I get back to the hotel, ignoring the stares of the hotel staff as I limp through the lobby, bruised and battered.

I return to my room and see Mary Sue's laptop open on my desk, right where we'd left it when we rushed out for our fateful rendezvous with Nick.

I don't know why, probably I just need something to keep my mind distracted, but I decide to pick up where Mary Sue and I left off and listen to the recording of the Town Hall meeting.

I scroll forward past the first few minutes of the meeting, anticipating it to be mostly small talk and pleasantries. I select a random point, about five minutes into where the recording devices started registering voices in the Town Hall meeting room, and Don Anderson's gruff voice booms out of the laptop's speakers, mid-sentence:

" . . . *the tournament next week's gonna be Texas Hold 'Em rules, boys, so that's what we're playin'. Any questions?*"

The other voices murmur understanding. I listen to a few more seconds, but it becomes immediately clear that we—Mary Sue, myself, Zeke, T.H.E.M., the Tennessee governor—have all been duped. It *was* just a poker game, all along.

I send Zeke a text message, asking exactly who the governor's informant was, though I have a sneaking suspicion. I hadn't asked before now, because I never figured it mattered who exactly it was that tipped off the governor that the Anderson men were involved with the K.K.K. But now . . .

A few minutes later, I receive a reply text from Zeke: 'Becky Grobes.'

The pieces of the puzzle all fit together as my suspicion is confirmed. Tired of being abused and taken advantage of, Becky Grobes it seems tipped off the governor a lie about her husband being involved in the K.K.K. in hopes it would get him locked up. No doubt, there was enough evidence of race-based violence in the pasts of Grobes and the Andersons that no one considered to question her claim.

I text Zeke back, informing him we've been played, that Becky fed the governor false information to save herself from an abusive marriage. Almost immediately, I receive a response:

'Terminate mission. Clean up loose ends immediately, and return to L.A. no later than tomorrow evening. Confirm receipt IMMEDIATELY.'

I read over the message. 'Clean up loose ends.' Per T.H.E.M.'s standard operating procedure, I know without a doubt what he means. I must eliminate any possible lines of exposure for T.H.E.M.—anyone involved in the mission that Mary Sue and I had extensive contact with over the course of the assignment. In other words, Clark Jr. and Duke Anderson.

I text back, 'Confirm. But what about Clark Sr.?'

'Unless he is a risk of exposure, DO NOT ELIMINATE. Am I clear?'

I bite back the bile building in my throat, and reply, 'You are clear.'

My heart feels heavy, but I know what I must do, for my own sanity and closure, not to mention in honor of Mary Sue's memory. I've disobeyed orders from Zeke in the past, but I always knew what lines not to cross. Murdering someone I have been given express orders not to kill would be one of those lines.

But for the first time in my long, bloody career, I am going to take a risk that likely will end that very career.

Even though I have no valid reason to want to kill Clark Grobe—he was innocent of the accusations lodged against him, after all. But after everything that has happened over the last week, this is something I have to do for myself—and for Mary Sue as well. I know after listening to the tapes of Clark abusing Becky, Mary Sue wanted him dead as much as I did. This transgression will be my way of honoring her memory—a kill we would have done together, if we could have.

And if this means I will be disavowed by T.H.E.M., then so be it.

31

I WAIT UNTIL midnight, and then make the drive out to Bucksnort, my plan fully formed, all the while praying I don't cross the path of a speed trap and wind up in a radar-induced coma.

I go to Duke's apartment first, as his murder will be the simplest to take care of, since he lives alone. Using my trusted lock pick, I break into his apartment for the second time this week. I'm glad I was the one who bugged Duke's apartment, because having a mental image of the apartment's layout helps me navigate my way through it in the dark.

I tiptoe down the hall to Duke's bedroom, and enter to find him, snoring lightly on the bed. I cross the room and kneel by the bed. As I look at him sleeping so peacefully, I start to wonder if I will actually be able to go through with this.

I put my knife down on the edge of the bed, and reach over to stroke his hair. Duke suddenly wakes with a start.

"Jesus, Nanny!" he gasps. "You scared the shit out of me, what are you doing here?"

"I'm sorry," I whisper, "I found out I have to leave tomorrow for a new project, and I just wanted to see you one more time before I left."

"Why didn't you call? How did you get—"

I don't let him finish, because I know I have no good answers for his questions, and so I cut him off by kissing him full and hard.

As he kisses me back, I wait for the urge to overcome me, the urge to kill him but it doesn't come. Not extracting myself from his lips, I roll over my knife onto the bed, getting more comfortable until the urge finally comes.

Dukes hands start to roam, massaging my thigh through my jeans and . . . *there* it is. Finally, I was starting to think I'd actually have to start having sex before the urge came. That would have just been awkward, not to mention the extra work I'd have to do to make sure I didn't leave any incriminating DNA behind . . .

Making sure I act before the urge fades away again, I grab the knife from my side and plunge it into Duke's throat, severing his vocal cords and preventing him from being able to scream.

"I'm sorry," I whisper into his ear, as his eyes bulge with shock and horror, and I mean it. "I feel like I owe you the truth. I'm not a legal aid. I'm a contract serial killer for hire. I was sent here to kill you and your family, because my agency was fed false information about you being White Supremacist Nazis. Unfortunately, even though I found out those allegations were false, I'd already built a relationship with you by that point, and I have to clean up all loose ends before I leave. I hope you understand."

I can tell from the look of betrayal in his eyes he does not understand even a little bit, but I am glad to say I feel no remorse as I watch the life drain from his face. Finally, I am back to my normal, heartless self. It seems Nanetta and all her redeeming qualities died in the church with Mary Sue. Thank porcupines for small favors.

I wait until I am certain there is no life remaining in him, and then leave. This part of the story I have not created a viable Herring for. It's unusual for me, but I suppose this is my tribute to Mary Sue—how she'd preferred her assassin's way of killing and disappearing, leaving no story to cover her tracks, over my P.S.K. method of always providing a story to hide my identity. It feels oddly fitting that I'm taking Mary Sue's lead for Duke's death.

The Grobes will be a bit more difficult to pull off, due to them all living under one roof, but at least I have my Herring story all planned out for them. There are more variables for something to go wrong, but I admit the risk makes it more exciting.

Ten minutes after leaving Duke's apartment, I pull into the Grobes's driveway and cut the headlights. I break into the house, and contemplate where to go first. I decide to first go to the basement and find Clark Jr. Unfortunately, since Mary Sue bugged this house, I've lost the benefit I had in Duke's apartment, and have to tread a little more carefully as I search my way through the darkness to find the entrance to the basement.

Just outside the kitchen, I find the door which hides the descending staircase, and slowly make my way down, one step at a time, hoping a creaky floorboard doesn't give my approach away.

After what seems like an eternity, I reach the bottom, and by now my eyes have adjusted to the darkness. Even so, I hear Clark Jr.'s snores before I see him. Across the room, I can just make out a large dark shape against the wall—a pullout sofa which Clark Jr. apparently calls his bed.

I cross to the sofa bed, kneel down, and cover Clark Jr.'s mouth with my hand before plunging the knife into his gut (not having developed an emotional relationship with him, I do not feel the need to wait for the urge as I did with Duke). Clark Jr.'s eyes open wide in shock, and I feel the reverberation of his scream against the palm of my hand, but hardly any sound escapes.

I lean in and whisper, "Unfortunately, Lindsay couldn't be here to do this herself, but believe me, she wanted to. Oh, and that reminds me," I stab again, this time into his groin, relishing the pain flashing in his eyes, "the clitoris is not in the belly button, you fucking jackass."

I stab him a few more times to make sure I damage enough organs to do the job thoroughly, and remain at his side, my hand clamped over his quivering mouth, until I feel no more breath, and no more beating of his heart.

I wipe the blood and guts off of my knife, then make my way back upstairs. I return outside to the car, open up the trunk and carry Mary Sue's corpse into the house. For a tiny bimbo, she sure as fuck is heavy . . .

I leave her, for now, in the living room and make my way down the hallway—I assume the master bedroom will be the one at the end of hall, but I check the first room, just to be sure; Tim's room. The teenager is sleeping soundly, and I close the door, leaving him undisturbed. The next room down looks like a storage room, and across from that room is a bathroom. As I assumed, the master bedroom is the last room in the hallway.

I take out my phone and dial Zeke's personal number.

"Sarah, what the hell–" Zeke starts, but I mute him and turn the phone on speaker, so he can hear everything that is about to happen, but no one else in the house will be able to hear him.

I stash my phone in my pocket, and tiptoe into the Grobes's bedroom. Clark Sr. is snoring so loudly, it's a fucking wonder he doesn't wake himself up. Honestly, it's a good thing he doesn't live in a coastal community, 'cause he'd probably cause a fucking tsunami or something. It sounds like a fucking walrus being strangled alive with a lynx-gut-piano-wire by a constipated polar bear (don't ask how I know what that sounds like . . . in my years with T.H.E.M., I've seen things no one should have to see . . .)

I follow the sound of the snores to the bed and look down at the couple. I seriously wonder how Becky can stand to sleep in the same bed as this pig, even if he isn't the White Supremacist she made him out to be.

Wanting to get this over with quickly and painlessly, I ram my knife into Clark Sr.'s throat. As he gasps awake, sputtering blood, Becky's eyes bolt open and she screams when she sees the macabre scene playing out in her bed.

"For fuck's sake, shut up," I hiss at her, "unless you want to wake up Tim."

Her eyes look like they're going to bulge straight out of their sockets, and she continues to whimper loudly, but she manages to stop screaming, so I gotta give her credit for that at least.

"W-who are you? Why are you d-doing this?" she sputters as she watches the life of her pig husband drain into the bed sheets.

"You told the Governor your asshole husband was in the K.K.K.," I state.

"How did you—"

"The governor contracted us to 'eliminate the threat.' Only problem, Becky, is we found out you were lying. That put us in a bit of a sticky situation, as my partner had already initiated contact with your louse of a son, Clark Jr., so before I can pull out of this bullshit assignment, I have to tie up all loose ends—namely, your son."

"C-Clark . . . "

"Just shut up and listen," I snap, not having the patience for dramatic grieving right now. "I know *why* you lied about your husband, and I couldn't in good conscience come into your home, take your son, and then leave you stuck with the bastard, so consider this a favor from me to you. I'm not one who frequently gives out favors, so you might as well take what you're gonna get here.

"There's a dead woman in your living room," I continue, ignoring Becky's sobs and whimpering. "In a few moments, I'm going to bring her in here. You can repay my favor to you by not calling the cops while I do that. After I'm gone, feel free to go ahead and call the cops. I would recommend you tell them the woman was sleeping with your husband, and when he tried to break off the relationship she went crazy and killed your son, your husband, and tried to kill you as well, but you killed her first. If you want to tell them the 'truth,' I certainly won't be able to stop you, but let me just say my people will be able to make your life so unpleasant that you'll wish I hadn't been so generous and left you with your abusive ass-hat of a husband alive. Understand?"

Shakily, Becky nods her head.

"Good girl," I say. "Five more minutes, and then you'll never see me again. That's a promise."

I leave her alone and carry Mary Sue's body back down the hall, reflecting on how fortunate that Tim seems to be, like most kids his age, a heavy sleeper. If my hunch about Zeke is correct, then it wouldn't be an unrecoverable problem if Tim did wake up to witness anything, but just in case my hunch is wrong, I'd rather not risk it.

I remove Nick's knife from Mary Sue's throat and hand it to the quivering Becky Grobes.

"Say when she came at you, you managed to get the knife away from her and used it against her. There's no legal defense like self defense. Good luck."

With that, I leave her to grieve, stab her husband a couple times herself, whatever the fuck she wants.

I get back into the Skank Mobile, and take Zeke's call off of mute.

"I presume you heard all of that, sweetie?" I say calmly, as I pull out of the Grobes' driveway.

"SARAH WHAT THE FUCK ARE YOU PLAYING AT?" Zeke screams, and even though I'm spared the full volume of his wrath by the speaker of my phone, I still get the message that he's not happy with me at this moment.

"I presume your mind control serum also gives you the ability to alter people's memories?" I reply, ignoring his question to get to the point.

"How do you know about th—*fuck*. Nick," he says, answering his own question (not to mention most of my own questions) as realization strikes. I hadn't told Zeke all of the details of Mary Sue's and my chat with Nick earlier in the evening—I wanted to wait until I was ready for the answers.

"Yes, Nick," I reply curtly. "I suggest you send the get the extraction team out here ASAP, because who knows how long Becky will wait before calling the cops."

"They're already on the way," he says, so quiet it's almost imperceptible.

I figured as much. I assumed as soon as Zeke heard me talking to Becky, he'd have the extraction team dispatched. I wasn't sure if they would be able to alter Becky's memory with the serum or not—but Zeke answered that question for me just fine. I might worry they would eliminate the problem by killing Becky, too, but as long as she doesn't stall before calling the cops, I doubt they'll have time for that. It'll be faster and cleaner for them to issue her the serum and replace her memory with the story I provided her.

"This is far from over, Sarah," Zeke hisses into the phone. In all the years I have known him, I have never heard him so dangerously angry, but I honestly don't care. If this leads to my being disavowed from T.H.E.M., I feel confident I have enough leverage to stop them from putting me into the slammer. Granted, the task of hunting down Nick's mysterious cohort would be a lot harder without T.H.E.M.'s resources, but if I have to find this bastard by myself, I will, with or without T.H.E.M.'s help.

"Oh, I know, Easy. You and I are going to have a

long talk when I get back to L.A. about this serum of yours. Sleep tight, Easy."

And without another word, I hang up and finish the drive back to Dickson.

Back in my hotel room, I strip and place all of my bloodied clothes into a sealed bag I will take back to L.A., and T.H.E.M.'s evidence disposal team will incinerate them when I report to headquarters.

Not having the energy to change into even pajamas, I climb into bed naked and fall almost instantly asleep. For the first time in over a week, my slumber is free of any dreams. It may have cost me the only friend I've ever had, but I am finally free from Nick Jin's raping of my subconscious.

In the morning, I wake up to see I have received a text message from Zeke, informing me of my departure flight information. No mention, of course, about anything else discussed the previous night. That conversation will wait until we are face-to-face.

I check out of the hotel, telling them 'Lindsay' and I have been reassigned to new projects, and she already left to catch a red eye flight late last night. The staff is sad to see us go—I'm sure they liked having guests who were quiet, didn't complain, and didn't get up to killing the other guests. I'll just have to save that for the next time I stay with them . . .

Zeke arranged for a town car to pick me up and take me to the airport—the extraction team reclaimed the evidence-strewn Skank Mobile in the middle of the night.

I go through the movements of checking into my flight and going through security, trying not to remind myself that Mary Sue is supposed to be here with me right now. On the trip here to Tennessee, I would have given anything to be alone and not have to listen to Mary Sue's chatter. Now, the absence of her babble only reminds me I will never see her again, and fills my already cold heart with ice.

Even though it's an early afternoon flight, and I usually don't sleep on planes, I'm so exhausted from the last twenty-four hours, that I doze with no problem for almost the entire flight—and it is a blissful, dreamless sleep. I almost had begun to think I'd never have a dreamless sleep ever again.

I wake as the flight's descent begins, and I decide the first thing I will do tomorrow morning, is pay a visit to my mother at L.A. County Prison. Not just because I missed getting to visit her before I left for Tennessee, but after everything that happened with Mary Sue, more than ever I feel the need to see my mother, possibly the only person left in the world who actually cares about me now that Mary Sue is dead.

After the flight lands and we are taxiing on the runway, I turn on my phone and immediately receive a notification that Zeke had texted me while I was in the air. Odd. What could he possibly have to tell me that couldn't wait until I come into headquarters? Did something go south with Becky's memory swipe?

I open the text, and read, "Call me as soon as you're alone. Whatever you do, DON'T LOOK AT THE NEWS."

I'm hurt. After all these years, Zeke should know

me better than that. If there was anything he could do to ensure I *will* look at the news, it's to tell me not to.

I pull up the news app on my phone, and almost immediately wish that, for once, I had listened to Zeke.

The top story depicts an aerial photograph of an oppressive black cloud of smoke emerging from an enormous crater where the L.A. County Prison should have stood, accompanied by the headline: *'Terrorist Bombing At L.A. County Prison, No Survivors.'*

With a sinking heart I realize, *my mother is dead.*

ABOUT THE AUTHOR

In addition to the *Sarah Killian* books, Mark Sheldon is the author of *The Noricin Chronicles* series and numerous published short stories. Mr. Sheldon lives in Southern California with his wife Betsy.

THE END?

Not quite . . .

Dive into more Tales from the Darkest Depths:

Novels:
Beatrice Beecham's Ship of Shadows: A Supernatural Adventure/Mystery Novel by Dave Jeffery
The Mourner's Cradle: A Widow's Journey by Tommy B. Smith
House of Sighs (with sequel novella) by Aaron Dries
Beyond Night by Eric S. Brown and Steven L. Shrewsbury
The Third Twin: A Dark Psychological Thriller by Darren Speegle

Novellas:
A Season in Hell by Kenneth W. Cain
Quiet Places: A Novella of Cosmic Folk Horror by Jasper Bark
The Final Reconciliation by Todd Keisling
Run to Ground by Jasper Bark
Devourer of Souls by Kevin Lucia

Anthologies:
Tales from The Lake Vol.5, edited by Kenneth W. Cain
Fantastic Tales of Terror: History's Darkest Secrets, edited by Eugene Johnson

Welcome to The Show, edited by Doug Murano
Lost Highways: Dark Fictions From the Road edited by D. Alexander Ward
C.H.U.D. Lives!—A Tribute Anthology

Short story collections:
Book Haven and Other Curiosities by Mark Allan Gunnells
Darker Days by Kenneth W. Cain
Dead Reckoning and Other Stories by Dino Parenti
Things You Need by Kevin Lucia
Frozen Shadows and Other Chilling Stories by Gene O'Neill

Poetry collections:
The Place of Broken Things by Alessandro Manzetti and Linda D. Addison
WAR by Alessandro Manzetti and Marge Simon
Brief Encounters with My Third Eye by Bruce Boston
No Mercy: Dark Poems by Alessandro Manzetti
Eden Underground: Poetry of Darkness by Alessandro Manzetti

If you've ever thought of becoming an author, we'd also like to recommend these non-fiction titles:

It's Alive: Bringing Your Nightmares to Life edited by Eugene Johnson and Joe Mynhardt
The Dead Stage: The Journey from Page to Stage by Dan Weatherer
Where Nightmares Come From: The Art of Storytelling in the Horror Genre edited by Joe Mynhardt and Eugene Johnson

Horror 101: The Way Forward, edited by Joe
Mynhardt and Emma Audsley
Horror 201: The Silver Scream Vol.1 and *Vol.2*,
edited by Joe Mynhardt and Emma Audsley

**Or check out other Crystal Lake
Publishing books for more Tales
from the Darkest Depths.**

Hi readers,

It makes our day to know you reached the end of our book. Thank you so much. This is why we do what we do every single day.

Whether you found the book good or great, we'd love to hear what you thought. Please take a moment to leave a review on Amazon, Goodreads, or anywhere else readers visit. Reviews go a long way to helping a book sell, and will help us to continue publishing quality books. You can also share a photo of yourself holding this book with the hashtag #IGotMyCLPBook!

Thank you again for taking the time to journey with Crystal Lake Publishing.

We are also on . . .

Website:
www.crystallakepub.com

Be sure to sign up for our newsletter and receive three eBooks for free: http://eepurl.com/xfuKP

Books:
http://www.crystallakepub.com/book-table/

Twitter:
https://twitter.com/crystallakepub

Facebook:
https://www.facebook.com/Crystallakepublishing/

Instagram:
https://www.instagram.com/crystal_lake_publishing/

Patreon:
https://www.patreon.com/CLP

Or check out other Crystal Lake Publishing books for more Tales from the Darkest Depths. You can also subscribe to Crystal Lake Classics (http://eepurl.com/dn-1Q9), where you'll receive fortnightly info on all our books, starting all the way back at the beginning, with personal notes on every release. Or follow us on Patreon (https://www.patreon.com/CLP) for behind the scenes access, bonus short stories, polls, interviews, and if you're interested, author support.

With unmatched success since 2012, Crystal Lake Publishing has quickly become one of the world's leading indie publishers of Mystery, Thriller, and Suspense books with a Dark Fiction edge.

Crystal Lake Publishing puts integrity, honor, and respect at the forefront of our operations.

We strive for each book and outreach program that's launched to not only entertain and touch or comment on issues that affect our readers, but also to strengthen and support the Dark Fiction field and its authors.

Not only do we publish authors who are legends in the field and as hardworking as us, but we look for men and women who care about their readers and fellow human beings. We only publish the very best Dark Fiction, and look forward to launching many new careers.

We strive to know each and every one of our readers while building personal relationships with our authors, reviewers, bloggers, podcasters, bookstores, and libraries.

Crystal Lake Publishing is and will always be a beacon of what passion and dedication, combined with overwhelming teamwork and respect, can accomplish: unique fiction you can't find anywhere else.

We do not just publish books, we present you worlds within your world, doors within your mind from talented authors who sacrifice so much for a moment of your time.

This is what we believe in. What we stand for. This will be our legacy.

Welcome to Crystal Lake Publishing.

THANK YOU FOR PURCHASING THIS BOOK!